Praise for

Black Wido

and for L

Gloria Dam

"Eighteen years ago, Licia Román Lec
her husband . . . Now that she's serve
called Black Widow seems to be mor
least that's how it seems to Oakland
Gloria's third [adventure] is part mystery, part history, part travelogue,
part spiritual speculation—a busy, many-layered invention stuffed
within an inch of its many lives."

—Kirkus Reviews

"Dark family secrets emerge and passionate sexual intrigues abound as
the story builds with a complexity worthy of a Ross MacDonald novel.
Woven through the narrative is the grim legacy of pesticide poisoning
suffered by farmworkers in the [California] Central Valley . . . A shattering conclusion, complete with the requisite gunplay, leaves the
reader eager for the next episode of this excellent homage to detective
fiction."

—San Francisco Chronicle-Examiner Book Review
on Cactus Blood

(please turn the page for more rave reviews)

Black Widow's Wardrobe

A Gloria Damasco Mystery

Featuring Gloria Damasco

Eulogy for a Brown Angel

Cactus Blood

Black Widow's Wardrobe

Also by Lucha Corpi

Delia's Song

Palabras de mediodía
(Noon Words)

Variaciones sobre una tempestad
(Variations on a Storm)

Black Widow's Wardrobe

Lucha Corpi

Arte Público Press
Houston, Texas
1999

This volume is made possible through grants from the City of Houston and the Texas Commission on the Arts through the Cultural Arts Council of Houston / Harris County.

Recovering the past, creating the future

Arte Público Press
University of Houston
Houston, Texas 77204-2174

Cover illustration and design by Vega Design Group

Corpi, Lucha
    Black widow's wardrobe / by Lucha Corpi.
    p.   cm.
    ISBN 1-55885-288-3 (pbk. : alk. paper)
    I. Title.
PS3553.0693B58   1999
813'.54—dc21   99-31948
                                                    CIP

♾ The paper used in this publication meets the requirements of the American National Standard for Information Sciences—Permanence of Paper for Printed Library Materials, ANSI Z39.48-1984.

9 0 1 2 3 4 5 6 7 8   10 9 8 7 6 5 4 3 2 1

In memoriam
José Antonio Burciaga

ACKNOWLEDGMENTS

My heart-felt gratitude to Pilar and Edgar at Rancho Digital in Yautepec, Morelos, for making my stay in their artists' colony not only very pleasant but fruitful as well. For reasons that will become obvious to the reader, I also thank my dear friends and partners in crime, Professors Norma Alarcón and Francisco X. Alarcón. To my publisher, Dr. Nicolás Kanellos, my indebtedness for pointing me in the direction of Tepoztlán and the Church of La Santísima, and for his insights. Special thanks to Mr. Darrell Ovid, former principal, and Ms. Dorothy Rogers, librarian, at Oakland Technical High School, for letting me visit the school and making its archives available, and to Mr. Carlos Gonzales, assistant principal at Fremont High School, for sharing his experiences as a former high-school dean of students. My appreciation to Robert Wells, fellow teacher, for the benefit of his suspicious mind during the writing of an earlier version of this book, and to my editor, Clifford Crouch, for his thoughtful and thorough editorial comments and suggestions. Last but not least, my deep gratitude to Marina Tristán, assistant director at Arte Público Press. Her friendship and her enthusiasm for, and belief in, my work have sustained me through the years.

* * * * * * * *

Although there are many caverns in the Ajusco Mountains and the Sierra of Tepoztlán, the caves depicted in this book are in their entirety products of my dark imagination.

L.C.

New Year's Eve, 1971, Midnight.

He sleeps now. My husband, Peter.

I don't know if I'll get through this night. Perhaps I will, as I have through many other painful, loveless nights in my life. Every time his hand strikes, every time he smells the panties of the lover he was with earlier and tells me I can never be like her, every time he forces me to get on my knees to prove to him I am as good a lover as she, I tell myself it would be so easy to die. But it isn't easy. I haven't the strength. He hasn't the strength to kill me either. He might, one day.

Oh, God. What sins have I committed that I must now gather this bitter harvest? Why can't I stop loving him? Why can't You save me from my love for him? When did You stop loving me?

March 21, 1972, Four o'clock in the morning.

Gone three days, but he's come back, a madman, God's Angel of Death.

Every night sound seems to whisper the name I'm trying to forget. Makes me remember the countenance I wish I had never held in my gaze, the hands that know only how to hurt me. But I can't feel anything anymore, not even the blows. I am beyond agony, beyond hope.

I sit in front of the open window. And I write, my last testament.

In the southern sky, the moon plots its course through a narrow strait between dark clouds. A dog barks. A relentless, sleepless mockingbird sings his undying song of love.

A gunshot shatters the quiet of the night. Someone dies out there, alone, her blood spilling over cold cement on a sidewalk, over kitchen tiles. I am she. And she I, alone, too.

God, love me a little. Give me the strength to do what I must. Don't stay my hand. Please.

[From the so-called "Black Widow's Diary,"
published in *The Wardrobe*, by Celia Howard
(New York: Freundlich Books, 1973)]

Not day anymore, not yet night, it is the hour of the wild cat, the ocelot. A woman fans the fire in a stone stove. She wears a mid-length skirt underneath a huipil with embroidered red flowers. Her long hair streams down her back. Her back is to me and I cannot see her face. Her young daughter plays by her side. A brooding young man sit at the kitchen table, playing with a dagger, a gift from his father. Suddenly, without saying a word, he gets up, picks up the dagger, and walks toward the woman at the stove. He raises his hand. She turns. The fire flares up, and her hair catches on fire, then her clothes. The kitchen fills with the stink of searing flesh and hair. Terrified, I do nothing to help her. I watch her burn until there is nothing but a pile of smoking bones. I flee into the darkness, and run and run until I can go no more.

The first time I laid eyes on Black Widow, walking down a dark street in the Mission District, I knew she was the woman in my recurring nightmare. Two days later, I helplessly realized that my feelings and dreams had become inextricably meshed with the threads of Black Widow's life. I knew that the visions would follow, and that I would give myself no choice but to work toward freeing myself from their hold.

ONE
The Dark Wind

It was the second of November—the Day of the Dead. The northern wind, a cool breeze at dawn, had turned into a chilling gale by noon. It was still blowing steadily at seven-thirty that evening when my mother, my daughter Tania, and I crossed the Bay Bridge from Oakland to San Francisco and stepped into Mission Dolores in the Mission District. My mother insisted we pay our respects to our dead husbands at church first. Only then would she agree to join the procession.

We joined the candlelit Procession of the Dead as the marchers turned from Mission to Twenty-fourth Street, moving towards the Galería de La Raza. The procession was headed by Don Mariano Tapia and his *matachines*—dancers in Aztec dress— and Mexican *charros* on horseback, wearing death masks over their faces. Two of the horsemen held a Mexican and a U. S. flag respectively. They flanked one in the middle who carried a banner of the Virgin of Guadalupe. Along the way, a few San Francisco policemen, also on horseback, watched over the crowd.

Holding in our hands photos of my father, who died six years before, and my husband, dead four years already, we joined a group of mourners. They too all displayed in some fashion pictures of their deceased relatives and friends.

Many of us were clad in black. But not the woman a few feet away from us. She wore a long, pleated, white dress. A white, waist-length poncho of wool covered her shoulders and torso. Unrestrained by band or comb, her glossy dark hair hung loosely down her back to her waist.

Behind us marched a group of acrobats and actors from Bay Area theater groups. On their tight, long-legged, black body suits

1

and head wraps were painted the bones of the skeleton and skull. Some of the group performed acrobatic stunts while others interacted with the observers lining the sidewalks.

The merry-makers, on the other hand, were dressed in colorful costumes which seemed more appropriate for Halloween than for a Day of the Dead procession. But mourners and revelers alike debated whether to hold their masks in place or cup their hands around the fluttering flames to keep the dark wind from blowing their candles out. All of us closed rank to keep the cold blade of the wind from cutting through skin and flesh down to our *real* bones.

As I breathed in the fragrance of fresh flowers coming from the woman in white, I realized the crowd had pushed us closer to her. I observed the photo and the bouquet of marigolds she was holding. It seemed fitting that she carry the marigolds—*cempoalxuchitls*—since these are the flowers of the dead in Mexican tradition. But whose photo did she hold? She turned her head once, slightly, as if she detected my curiosity.

Perhaps, like me, she had recently lost her husband. I had to fight my impulse to comfort her, to tell her that in time we learn to live with the pain and we go on. But the voice of reason in me whispered a warning. I took heed and withheld my comforting hand.

When we reached the Galería, my mother, Tania, and I looked at the altars and the boxed *ofrendas* for the dead there. At a theater nearby we heard our poet friends Francisco Alarcón, Art Bello, Myra Miranda, and others recite *calaveras,* biting, humorous commentaries in verse form, written especially for this day. Later, in the company of the poets, we had *pan de muertos* and hot chocolate at a bakery and cafe a few blocks from the old York Theater.

As we sat there talking, the woman in white came into the cafe. Everyone looked up as she entered. Everyone hushed. Oblivious to the attention, she sat in a far corner, facing the other customers.

"Wow!" Myra whispered.

I could finally see the woman's face and I tried to observe her without staring. At least five-feet-six, and of medium build, she seemed self-possessed to the point of aloofness. Her eyes, framed by arched brows and prominent cheekbones, were large and observant, and they animated an otherwise doleful countenance. I tried inconclusively to guess her age.

"She was in the procession," Tania said. "She looks so sad."

"Sad but lovely," Art commented. "She is . . . regal in her sadness. Like a tragic Greek heroine."

"More like a tragic Aztec princess," Francisco remarked.

"More like a brown murderess," Myra said.

"That's an odd thing to say," I murmured, my curiosity piqued.

"You really don't recognize her, Gloria?" Myra asked. "Her picture ran in the Bay Area newspapers almost every day, back around 1972. The press had a field day. They called her Black Widow. She killed her husband. She said he had 'physically and sexually abused' her. She was only twenty-four when she killed him. She just got out of prison. A while back, the paper ran a short article rehashing the case when she came up for parole."

"Now that you mention it, I did read that article." I said.

"Have you seen that beautiful old Victorian house on East Twenty-seventh Street, near Highland Hospital in Oakland?" Myra asked.

"That's the scene of the crime—*his* crime."

"How do you know so much about this?" I inquired.

"My friend Celia Howard, the *Tribune* reporter and mystery writer, wrote a book about the case, *The Wardrobe*. I helped her edit it for publication," Myra explained.

"Are you sure that woman is her?'" my mother asked.

"She sure is," Myra said with a nod. Turning to me, she added, "You can borrow the book if you like, Gloria."

"I'll take you up on that. Thanks."

Quietly, but with avid eyes, the woman in white watched everything around her. I suppose after eighteen years inside a prison, everything must have seemed new to her, and odd at times perhaps.

Finishing her meal, Black Widow left some money on the table then rose to her feet. Many eyes, including mine, followed her as she walked into the night, whispers, murmurs, and gusts of dark wind trailing close behind her.

TWO
Horsemen Pass By

It was almost eleven by the time my mother, Tania, and I started back to our car, parked several blocks away. My mother leaned on my arm for support as we walked. Tania danced a few steps ahead of us.

The wind had waned to breaths of chilled air, and the ocean mist was creeping inland. We could hear music, voices, and laughter coming from the many restaurants and bars along Twenty-fourth Street. But, with the exception of cars cruising towards Mission Street or an occasional drunk staggering out of a bar, the streets were deserted. Since it was a Friday night, I assumed that all the marchers, particularly the merry-makers and poets, were dancing death away at the *Centro Chicano de Escritores's* Rhythm and Rhyme Costume Ball.

"Not quite everyone," I whispered when I saw the woman in the white dress walking with unhurried steps towards Balmy Street, about fifty feet ahead of us.

I caught sight of a patrol car cruising down South Van Ness. The fog-muffled sound of hoofs on the pavement echoed in the distance; the mounted police we had seen earlier were still at large.

Suddenly I heard the clatter of galloping hoofs. The noise stopped. In its echo I heard someone running. The hoofs resumed their gallop: The mounted officers were in pursuit of someone. Why were they, and not the black-and-whites, doing the pursuing?

I felt my mother's hand squeeze my arm. Tania waited until we caught up to her, then wrapped both her hands around my other arm.

"There's trouble ahead," I said. "Let's turn left at the corner and cut through Balmy. It connects with Twenty-fifth Street. The car's about two blocks up. Hurry."

The woman in white walked faster, too, and turned onto Balmy ahead of us.

The darkness blinded us. Only a shaded light in a nearby window and a single street lamp at the other end of Balmy provided dim illumination, obscuring the bright murals that decorated the street's walls.

I stopped for a moment to give my eyes a chance to adjust. Looking around cautiously, I took a few hesitant steps, my mother and daughter in tow. The woman in white continued walking up the street relentlessly.

"Someone's watching us," Tania said, sucking in breath.

"Yes," my mother agreed. "Look at this place. There are so many doorways where a mugger or a rapist can hide." Her voice betrayed no apprehension but the grip on my arm tightened.

Black Widow stopped in the middle of the street with her back to us, her arms stretched out, and her head slightly thrown back. Her dress was so white it glowed in the darkness.

"*Es la llorona,*" my mother said, referring to the centuries-old Mexican legend of the woman who drowned her children and whose soul had been condemned to roam the world eternally in search of them.

"It can't be La Llorona, Mother. She didn't kill her children. She only killed her husband."

"Spooooky!" Tania said. Tugging on my sleeve, she asked, "What is she *doing*, Mom?"

The sound of galloping horses resumed abruptly; trouble was heading our way. I was about to suggest a quick retreat when we saw another woman, dressed in black, running towards Black Widow from the opposite direction, two mounted officers at her heels. She ran past Black Widow and then stopped. The horses slowed down, snorting.

Black Widow dropped her arms and took a step forward. She stretched her right arm in front of her, the palm of her hand out as if commanding the officers to halt. They did.

My mother and Tania moved behind me. I wasn't sure whether the horsemen were aware of our presence there. I pushed gently on my mother and daughter, and we stepped back until all three of us were pressed against the wall. The darkness my mother had so dreaded a while back now gave us refuge.

One of the riders pulled on his reins. His horse reared for a few seconds, while the other whinnied.

The fugitive woman stood a few feet away from us. Her face was covered with white make-up, her mouth agape. The vapor of her quick breaths danced in the cold night air. She rested her hands on her knees and lowered her head as she looked in all directions. Then she began to sob. My mother and daughter stirred behind me.

The fugitive woman looked in our direction. "Please, help me," she implored. "Please . . . This can't be happening. Please!"

Torn between my desire to help and my fear, I said, in a low voice, "Run. Get away." But she didn't move.

The woman looked in the direction of Black Widow and abruptly let out a long cry. I looked up the street and saw the horsemen start up—this time towards Black Widow. She stood her ground. I felt the prick of fear on my earlobes, then the back of my neck.

The fugitive woman fled. The horses stepped up their pace too. In terror, I saw the horsemen coming towards her and us. Out of the corner of one eye, I saw a shadow step out of a doorway, close to Black Widow. I saw someone peer out from behind a window. As the riders passed under the window, I realized that they were not wearing San Francisco police uniforms. They were dressed as conquistadors. It was as if we had been caught in a time warp. As the riders maneuvered around Black Widow, she fell to the ground. My mother and daughter and I pressed our backs to the wall as the horses flew past, the fog swirling behind them.

Leaving the protection of the wall, I took a few shaky steps forward. I watched the horsemen close in on the fugitive woman. They reached down and pulled her up by her arms, then turned the corner, disappearing with their squirming, wailing cargo.

Everything had happened so fast that I now stood in the middle of the street, panting but paralyzed. My mother and daughter stared at me, frozen in shock. I hugged them and rubbed their arms and the nape of their necks to speed up the flow of blood. Following my example, they started to rub each other's arms.

I turned around and looked in the direction of Black Widow. She lay motionless on the ground. As I began to move towards her, I caught sight of someone standing at the other end of the street, watching us: someone in tight, black skeletal costume and headdress, the phosphorescent skull, ribs, arms, and legs still glowing. The acrobat did a somersault, landed gracefully with arms stretched out, took a bow, and ran away.

"Wait here," I told my mother and daughter. The woman in white lay flat on her back. In the darkness only half of her brown, oval face was visible. Her long hair lay in disarray over her chest.

I reached out to her neck and found her pulse. She opened her eyes briefly, then shut them again. A barely audible moan came from her. But the pungent smell of warm blood reached my nostrils. A large dark stain, still widening, spread over the whiteness of her dress just above her left breast. She had been stabbed.

Apprehension and fear tightened into a knot in my chest as I looked around, terrified. I had left my cellular phone in my car, but I remembered seeing a phone around the corner, on Twenty-fourth Street.

Tania knelt before the woman. With a trembling hand, she reached for the woman's wrist and felt her pulse.

"Let's go call the police," I said.

"We can't leave her here like this," my mother argued, clearing her throat.

"I won't leave you two alone here," I said. "Whoever did this might come back."

"Grandma and I can go," Tania suggested.

"Out of the question," I said. "We all go find a phone."

At the corner, I got a 911 dispatcher on the line and briefly explained. As I answered the dispatcher's questions, I tried not to think of the other woman, the woman in black, and of the horsemen.

When we rushed to the spot where we had left Black Widow, she was gone. Afraid that she might collapse again, I ran ahead of my mother and Tania to the corner, hoping to catch a glimpse of her white dress. But she was nowhere to be seen.

We found my car and circled the area for several minutes, without success. Back on Balmy Street, an ambulance and the police had already arrived, and were inspecting the scene. After I gave them a detailed account of the events we had witnessed, two policemen stayed with us while the others searched for the woman in white.

"Any idea who the other woman was or what was happening?" one of the officers asked.

"None. I'm sorry," I answered. For the time being, I thought it was better not to give a name to the woman in white. Following my lead, my mother and daughter simply confirmed what I said.

An hour later, the officers told us we could go home.

"Did you have any officers on horseback here after the procession ended?" I asked the youngest of the officers.

He looked at his partner, then said, "I don't think so, ma'am. They were scheduled to report back to the stables at about nine o'clock."

"So the two horsemen I saw couldn't have been policemen."

"I'm sure they weren't," the officer confirmed. "Trouble-makers, most likely."

We said goodnight and headed towards the car.

"Hmmm," my mother said as she looked at the spot where the woman in white had collapsed. "Maybe she's not of this world, after all. I don't see any blood here."

THREE
Visions of Fire

Panting and bathed in cold sweat, I sat up in bed. The woman burned again and I had done nothing to help her. A sharp pain shot up my left leg to my belly, leaving me breathless for a few seconds.

I walked slowly to the bathroom, took a long shower, got dressed, and started my day earlier than usual. Trying to shake off the image of the burning woman, I got busy with errands, then took care of the paperwork that had begun to pile on my desk.

Towards the end of the day, I found myself still unable to extricate myself from the dream web or to dispell the disquieting, oppressive feeling in my chest every time I remembered the dream.

Vivid nightmares were not unusual for me. Over the years, I'd had so many that I had learned to free myself from their hold as soon as I opened my eyes. But sometimes I had other kinds of dreams, dreams that triggered visions, fragmented images, and symbols of a larger picture I felt compelled to put together. I dreaded that moment when my visions forced me to act on them. My *dark gift* was a mixed blessing at best, but it was a part of me, a part my reason always tried to deny or control.

Towards the end of the day, I phoned my partner Justin, the man with whom I had for some time shared my investigative work, my bed, and my dreams. He was in Los Angeles, working on another case; he had asked me to fax him some papers to a client's office there. After giving him a brief report on our activities in Oakland, I told him about the night before and what Myra had told me about Black Widow.

"I vaguely remember hearing about the Black Widow case at

the time," Justin said. "Did you talk to the San Francisco police?"

"Yes. They checked the area. They did find blood spots. The trail ended somewhere around the Bay Area Rapid Transit Station on Mission and Twenty-fourth. They think she got on a BART train headed towards the East Bay."

"Any idea who the other woman was—the one in black?"

"None. The police haven't the faintest either. And no one has reported an injured woman answering to Black Widow's description," I explained.

"And you already checked with hospitals in San Francisco and Oakland?"

"I haven't yet. I wanted to get our work out first. But I'll get to it as soon as we hang up."

Justin paused, then said, "I assume you're going to pursue this."

"Only to find out what happened to this woman."

"You know where to reach me," he said. He paused then added, "I've missed you very much."

"I have, too."

My conversation with Justin finished, I began a journey through the electronic maze of San Francisco and Oakland hospital voice mail systems, listening to complicated directions and punching numbers, finally getting through to human beings only to be put on hold again. I hated to think how I'd feel if I were a recent immigrant trying to get medical help. Every so often, voices in Spanish and Chinese offered help. But I wondered how the patients who spoke other languages—almost eighty in Oakland—managed.

Finally I decided to make inquiries at Oakland emergency rooms in person. Two hours of frustration later, I called Myra Miranda to borrow the book that her friend Celia Howard had written about Black Widow. But Myra had gone to San Jose to visit her family and wasn't expected back for a couple of days.

Unwilling to wait, I went to four bookstores in Berkeley and Oakland, but *The Wardrobe* had been out of print for a number of years.

On my way home, I took a quick detour and drove by the old house in Oakland that I'd been told had been the home of Black Widow in 1972. The great Victorian was imposing. An architectural relic predating the 1906 earthquake, it stood three stories high, looking pale against an unusually clear night and starry sky. Sitting on the brow of an Oakland foothill, it overlooked Lake Merritt and the bay. It rose taller than the old Highland Hospital's architectural twin towers. The house stood in darkness, except for the feeble light from an open attic window. I wondered if Black Widow still called it home.

FOUR
Past Selves, Past Sins

After my husband Darío died and my daughter Tania moved to Berkeley, the most troublesome day of the week for me became Sunday—Sunday afternoon in particular. I used to roam the house all morning, my anxiety and restlessness increasing with each hourly chime of the grandfather clock in my office.

Every Sunday, near two o'clock, my anxiety metastasized into depression, and I fled the house in search of a friend, a movie, a theater matinee, or anything else that would distract me for five hours. About eight o'clock in the evening, I would regain my composure and return home.

When Justin Escobar and I began working together, my Sundays became more pleasant and purposeful. But this Sunday, November 4, was different. With Justin in Los Angeles, and facing the prospect of another dreary Sunday afternoon, I decided to try to reach Celia Howard. Fortunately, she was listed in the phone book.

After I had explained my reasons for calling, she agreed to meet me at Scott's, in Jack London Square, for a drink. I sensed that she was as eager as I to talk about the case and intrigued by my brief description of Friday night's events.

A petite woman, poised and attractive, with bright hazel eyes, a quick wit, and an engaging smile, Celia arrived at three o'clock sharp. Without preamble she said, "I have to warn you: I don't know much more than what I wrote in *The Wardrobe*."

I explained that I hadn't read her book yet, that the bookstores where I'd looked for it no longer carried it, and that Myra, who owned a copy, was out of town.

Celia laughed. "It wasn't a bestseller, for sure, although it sold

well for a while. But I came prepared for that eventuality."
Reaching into her large handbag, she took out a slim hardcover
volume. "Here," she said. "It's yours. I marked those pages or sec-
tions you might want to concentrate on."

"That's wonderful. Thank you so much."

"Don't thank me yet. The information in it might not help
you at all."

"The life of Black Widow," I said as I flipped through the
pages. Amazing, how a lifetime of feelings, actions, and memories
could be compressed into a book, like ashes into a small burial
urn.

"As far as I'm concerned, the whole trial was a joke. Licia
Román Lecuona had been convicted even before her case went to
trial," Celia commented.

Without meaning to, I repeated, "Licia Román Lecuona."

"A pretty name, isn't it?"

"I gather that Lecuona was her husband's name."

I took Celia's nod as a *yes*, meaning that Román was Black
Widow's maiden name.

"Peter Percy Lecuona was a terrible man; I really believe that,"
Celia said, a hint of anger in her gaze and voice. "He married
Licia for her money, and then went on to abuse her physically as
well as emotionally. He spent a large part of her trust on dope,
alcohol, and hopeless financial schemes, not to mention the lavish
gifts he gave to the many women he had. I also think that the
Lecuonas ended up with quite a bit of that money, too."

"The Lecuonas?"

The barmaid approached with our drinks, and I took care of
the tab. Celia raised her glass and I mine.

"Peter was the grandson of a Spanish count, long dead," Celia
explained. "The Lecuonas left Spain in the 1930s, during that
country's civil war. They still held noble title and airs, but they no
longer had the money for their social aspirations. You can imagine how thrilled they were when Peter married Licia."

"Where was Licia's family while this was going on? Why
didn't they do something to help her?" I asked.

Celia shook her head. "Both her parents were dead. When Licia was three years old, her father, driven by jealousy—unfounded, as far as I can tell—shot Licia's mother, then blew his brains out. The child was in the room and saw it all. I suppose her grandmother, her father's mother, with whom Licia went to live after the murder-suicide, thought that a child that age would hardly remember such tragic events. I believe Licia was deeply affected by what she witnessed. Wouldn't anyone be?" she asked.

I agreed with a nod.

"Then," Celia continued, "her grandmother died when Licia was twenty. As far as I could tell, she had no other relatives. None came forward for a share of the grandmother's money—and certainly none came forward to support Licia after she killed her husband."

"What about her lawyer? Wasn't there any kind of a defense?"

"Lester Zamora was a public defender with only a few years experience," Celia said. "The court had no choice. Licia confessed to the murder voluntarily. She actually called the police and said she had done it. Her confession notwithstanding, she had to be represented by counsel during the arraignment and sentencing. That's the law. But Licia refused to even consider other criminal attorneys. Lester was appointed because he was the only one that Licia would accept. He tried his best, I must say. But he had a fool for a client.

"He convinced Licia to plead not guilty by reason of temporary insanity. The court appointed a psychiatrist who found her mentally competent. Strike one. Then he introduced evidence that was used against Licia. The most devastating evidence was her diary.

"An astute prosecutor used that information to prove that Licia had planned the murder days before it happened. Strike two. Then Lester tried to prove that Licia had been constantly abused by Peter. You see, when the police came to the house the night of the murder, they found Licia hiding in a wardrobe in the attic."

"A wardrobe," I interjected.

"Yes. The wardrobe had belonged to Licia's grandmother,"

Celia explained. "In it, the police found a nightgown with fresh bloodstains on it—Peter's. But they also found an assortment of evening dresses and a wedding gown hanging in it. The other gowns, including the wedding dress, also had old bloodstains on them, but they were identified as Licia's. Lester introduced the contents of the wardrobe as evidence, claiming the blood-stained dresses were proof of Peter Lecuona's physical abuse of his wife. Licia, however, had never reported it to the police.

"Apparently, there was also sexual abuse. Lester Zamora also tried to convince the jury that Peter had sexually abused Licia. But, again, at that time, the courts had not ruled that a husband could commit the crime of rape against his own wife. When a husband forced himself on his wife, the act wasn't seen as a rape.

"At any rate, with no help from Licia, who refused to testify in her own behalf, Zamora decided to base his defense on what we now call 'battered wife syndrome.' Zamora was a man ahead of his time, I must say. But he had no witnesses and no medical records to substantiate his allegations."

"Let me guess," I said. "The prosecutor brought in a number of witnesses who testified that Peter was a good man who loved his wife."

"You got it: Strike three. Twenty years in prison."

"And Lester Zamora lost his first big criminal case," I remarked. "How did he take losing? He must have been angry."

"He took it hard, of course. But, as I said, it really was not his fault."

"Where is Lester Zamora now? Do you know?"

"As a matter of fact, I do," she answered promptly. "I saw him recently at the opening of an art gallery in downtown Oakland. He's a partner in Stanley, Cartier and Foreman, here in Oakland."

"Does he know that Licia is out?"

"He told me so himself. You know what hurt him most?"

"What?"

Celia shook her head. "Licia was pregnant at the time of her trial, but kept the fact from Lester and everyone else."

"*What?*"

"Yep. Pregnant. Lester swears that he could have gotten her acquitted or else convicted of manslaughter, had he known about her condition. But I . . ."

"You don't think so."

"The jury—an all-male jury, by the way—and the press were out to get her. She didn't help matters much either."

"What happened to Licia's child?"

"Licia agreed to give the baby up for adoption. But a few days after birth, the baby died. It had been born with a heart defect."

"Is there . . . is there anything about Licia's life in prison in your book?" I asked.

"Not really," Celia said and paused. She was lost in thought for a moment, then continued, "Licia Lecuona never wanted to grant me any interviews until years later."

"I gather you visited her in prison. When was the last time you talked to her?"

"About three years ago. Licia seemed changed. She looked older, of course, but there was something else, something in the way she carried herself, perhaps. I'm really not sure. But she was a lot more open, happier . . . well, maybe less tortured. Mind you, she still didn't want to answer any questions about her husband's murder," Celia said and paused. A minute later, she asked, "Do you believe in reincarnation, Gloria?"

My first reaction was to say that I didn't. But there had been a time when I hadn't believed in clairvoyance, either. To Celia, I said, "I don't really know. I suppose I believe in the possibility."

"I know what you mean. There *are* times when I wish I did. I'd love to come back as a tall redhead with green eyes like Maureen O'Hara's, and the smarts of Gloria Steinem. Wishful thinking, huh?" Celia said and laughed. "Well, *Licia Lecuona* believes in reincarnation. Or so she told me when I visited her in prison."

"Was this something new? Or did she believe she was a rein-carnated soul when she was married to Peter Lecuona?" I asked.

"It's hard to tell," Celia said. "And there's nothing about it in her diary. But when I saw her in prison, she . . . well, she didn't say whose reincarnation she is in her present life—not exactly . . . But she did ask me to get some books for her."

"Books on reincarnation?"

"No. They all had to do with the history of Mexico, pre- and post-Conquest," Celia said. "I had Cody's Books in Berkeley send them to her. She also asked me to get in touch with a woman, a private investigator." Celia flipped through the pages of her memo book. "Here it is. Dora Saldaña. She was working—might still be working—with Ace Security and Investigations Agency in San Leandro. Do you know her?"

"No. I know about Ace Investigations, though. My partner, Justin Escobar, and the man who heads Ace have had some run-ins. But why did she want you to find Dora Saldaña?"

"I haven't the slightest. The message Licia sent to the private eye was, 'I have some additional information. Please come to see me as soon as you can.'"

"Do you have any idea where Licia is now?" I asked.

"Not exactly, but I assume she's living in her house on East Twenty-seventh. Where else would she go?" Remembering something, Celia added, "Come to think of it, there's someone who might know, but he's a very busy man and difficult to get hold of. His name is Michael Cisneros."

"The Oakland industrialist?" I asked.

"The same," Celia replied. "Do you know him? Of *course* you know him. I remember now. Didn't you and your partner work on the Cisneros child's murder? I didn't cover that case, but my husband did for the *Examiner*."

I marveled at her keen memory. "Yes, Justin and I found out who killed Michael Junior," I answered. "But what role did Michael Cisneros play in Licia Lecuona's case?"

"No role other than being the executor of Licia's grandmother's will. He managed Licia's business affairs until she married Peter Lecuona. Her grandmother had specifically requested that half of her inheritance be given to Licia when she turned twenty-one. The other half was to be given to her on her thirtieth birthday. By then, Licia was already serving her sentence. For all we know, Michael Cisneros might have continued handling business matters for Licia after she went to prison."

Las vueltas que da el mundo, my grandmother, Mami Julia, used to say whenever someone came into her life again at a most improbable time. I felt that way upon hearing Michael Cisneros' name. I scribbled his name along with those of Lester Zamora and Dora Saldaña.

"Do the Lecuonas still live in Oakland?" I asked.

"I don't think so. Last I knew about them, they moved to Cuernavaca, about . . . oh, fifteen, maybe sixteen years ago. But Peter's sister lives in Berkeley. I believe she's married to an anthropology professor. I think his name was—is—Juan Gabriel Lengo . . . No . . . Wait . . ." She flipped through the pages of her organizer: "Juan Gabriel Legorreta." I wrote that down, too.

Still dreading being alone in my house on this cloudy and cold Sunday afternoon, I went into the bookstore in Jack London Square and found a few books on reincarnation, one penned by a noted psychologist. For the next hour or so, I sat on a bench at the bookstore and read. I became aware that a whole school of psychologists believed in using therapy techniques based up on "regression to previous existences." Unusual behavior, idiosyncracies for which one has no explanation, bad habits—from nail-biting to hard drinking—were attributable to a previous self. Under hypnosis, once that "past self" could be convinced that his or her actions were damaging the present self, the patient would show marked improvement.

I wasn't convinced. But in this case it made no difference what I believed. It mattered only that Licia Román Lecuona believed herself to be the reincarnation of someone. Who? The question swooped down, like a seagull into the cold, blue Pacific, fishing and coming back up empty.

FIVE
Progressive Past

I walked around the waterfront, debating whether to call Michael Cisneros. My first impulse had been to call him. But wondering how painful it would be for the both of us to see each other again, I decided against it.

Although Michael had sent some business clients our way, neither Justin nor I had talked to him or his wife for quite some time. Michael's life, like mine, had changed drastically after Justin and I uncovered the truth about his son's murder.

In the course of that investigation, my best friend, Luisa Cortez, had died as a result of a bullet meant for me. Michael had lost his son, and then his brother, who had been responsible for the child's death. His wife, Lillian, unable to cope, had twice attempted suicide, and Michael had been compelled to have her committed to a private institution.

Finally, at about six o'clock, I mustered up enough courage to phone Michael at his home.

"Gloria, what a nice surprise," he said.

After inquiring about Lillian's and his health, I briefly told him about the attempt on Licia Lecuona and my conversation with Celia Howard.

"Celia mentioned you were named by Mrs. Román as the executor of her will. She also told me that you took care of business matters for Licia Román Lecuona, after . . . Peter Lecuona died."

For a while, there was only static at the other end of the line. Then, Michael said, "Yes. Gabriela Román, Licia's grandmother, named me her executor. She and my father had been good friends and business associates at one time. And I did promise her that I would look after Licia's interests and welfare. I have no idea who might be trying to kill Licia. Do you?"

"No, I don't. But I think it's important that we find her soon. Do you know where she is now?"

"She's been living on East Twenty-seventh since her release," he informed me. "I advised her not to move back to that house. She needs to be done with the past. Now you say someone is trying to kill her." Michael paused briefly then said, "Let me make a phone call. Give me your number and I'll call you back as soon as I can."

I gave him my cellular number. Not having much else to do, I went into El Torito Restaurant and had an early dinner. Michael called as I was getting back into my car.

"I just left Licia," he said. "She has a shoulder wound, apparently not very deep. She's been taking care of the wound herself and doing a good job. She, of course, refuses to be treated by a physician. I can understand her reluctance. Any doctor would have to report her injury to the authorities."

"I agree. It's not the kind of injury one gets from slicing tomatoes or falling down the stairs," I said. "Does she know who's trying to kill her? Did she tell you?"

Michael didn't reply right away. "I asked her. I'm not certain she knows her assailant." He hesitated again. "What she told me made no sense to me."

"She spoke of her other lives, is that it?"

Michael was silent at the other end of the line, and I realized that I'd been presumptuous. I related what Celia Howard had told me about Licia's belief in reincarnation.

He listened in silence, then said, "As you might have guessed, Licia and I didn't have long personal conversations over the years. I always found it quite difficult to reach out to her. Long ago, I decided to take care of only her business concerns. Now, I'm beginning to think that I should have done more for her, paid more attention to her psychological needs, perhaps."

"Would you mind telling me what she just said to you?"

"No. Not at all. She asked me to get her a passport and traveler's checks. She wants to go abroad for a while," he said. "I reminded her that she had to report to her probation officer—that she could go back to jail if she left the country. She simply said, 'I know what happened now. Nothing and no one will stop me.' I pleaded with her to tell me what was on her mind. She wouldn't."

Michael paused again, then said, "I know that you and Justin are busy. I wonder if you could look into this matter for me. As always, I'll take care of your fee and expenses."

"Justin is in Los Angeles right now. I'll phone him the minute we hang up. I'll let you know. But I don't foresee any problem," I said.

"Thank you. My chauffeur will come by your house to drop a check off this evening, if you accept this case."

"Just one more question, Michael: Why did Licia hire a private investigator by the name of Dora Saldaña? She worked, or still works, for Ace Security and Investigations in San Leandro, as far as I know."

"Ah, yes. We hired ASI. to secure and patrol Licia's house in her absence. The house was vacant all these years, and there had been some break-ins. The neighbors told the police they suspected that the house was being used by drug addicts. We had ASI look into the matter before we notified the police. Ms. Saldaña was assigned to the case."

"Was there any truth to the neighbors' claim?"

"Yes. As a matter of fact, thanks to Ms. Saldaña's good work, the police made some arrests. We also had a security system installed and I hired a man, Carmelo, to live in the house and take care of the property. But Ms. Saldaña usually reported to my lawyer, and he, of course, to me. I had no idea she was in contact directly with Licia. But I'll have someone look into the matter for you."

"Great. Thank you," I said. I turned the phone off and started the car.

The moment I arrived home, I left a message for Justin at his hotel in Los Angeles. When he called back an hour later, as I expected, he left the decision entirely up to me. I phoned Michael

Cisneros back. He would be out of town until Thursday, he said; would I get in touch with his personal secretary in case I needed to contact him?

Later that evening, with a few logs burning in the fireplace, I began to read Celia Howard's *Wardrobe*. A few hours later, emotionally and physically exhausted, I went upstairs to my bedroom. I drew the curtains and laid down on my bed, fully clothed. An instant later, it seemed I was having the same dream. The burning woman. The woman was Licia Lecuona.

SIX
Another Journey

Reading excerpts from Licia's diary in *The Wardrobe* confirmed my belief that domestic violence is a kind of war, a covert war, with battles fought behind closed doors in bedrooms and kitchens.

My reviewing Licia's torturous relationship with her husband brought my own marriage into focus. Darío and I had had a good marriage. I'd never had to ask myself why I, an intelligent and well-educated woman, could still love an abusive husband who often came home intoxicated and belligerent and went on rampages, breaking or damaging everything dear to me. Darío hadn't once come home saturated with the sweat and perfume and taste of the woman he'd just been with, then forced me to perform sexual acts. I'd never begged God to "send Death to kill my love for my husband."

What did Licia think now? Did she still feel the rage that had driven her to kill Peter? Did she still keep a diary? Had she kept one while in prison?

Hoping that Lester Zamora had some answers to my questions, I looked up the address for the offices of Stanley, Cartier, and Foreman. I decided to pay him a visit at his office.

Lester Zamora's law firm had a suite at the Clorox Building in downtown Oakland. Despite the windy and cold weather, street jazz musicians played in the City Center Plaza, and a homeless man talked to himself as he gyrated amid the music and the wind. When I got near him, he stretched his hand out, and I gave him a Kennedy half-dollar. He bowed, then went on with his dancing.

As I pulled on my side of the door at the law offices, a tall, well-dressed black man in his mid-thirties pushed on his side of it.

"Good luck in court, Johnny Cartier," the receptionist, a woman in her late fifties, said. He turned briefly and smiled at her. Her eyes followed him until he stepped into the elevator. I looked at her name plate. She looked at me, and her eyes turned serious. Seeing the smile on my face, her gaze softened.

"You have every reason to be proud of him," I said.

She chuckled. "Is it that obvious?"

"To the mother of a twenty-two-year-old medical student at UC it is," I answered.

"Praise the Lord," she remarked. "What can I do for you?"

"My name is Gloria Damasco. I'd like to see Mr. Zamora."

"Do you have an appointment with him?"

"No, I don't, but it's a matter of great importance," I told her. "Personal," I added, then handed her my card.

She raised her eyebrows. Curiosity appeared in her eyes, but her tone remained professional as she repeated, "Personal."

I replied with a nod.

"Then it's better if you talk to his secretary. Mr. Zamora is with a client now."

She reached the other woman on the intercom phone. Emphasizing the words "private detective," she gave her my name. After a pause, she lowered her voice. "Yes. Another one. It's personal."

Another one. Was I yet another woman with a personal problem looking for Lester Zamora? Another private investigator? Who had been here before me?

"She'll be with you momentarily. You may wait there if you like." She pointed to a nicely furnished waiting room, with oil paintings decorating the walls and plush carpeting muting footsteps and voices. Lester Zamora had done well for himself, but his name wasn't yet stenciled on the door, I thought as I sank into a cushiony armchair and began to leaf through *San Francisco Focus*.

Fifteen minutes later, a woman stood in front of me. "Gloria Inés Vélez?" she asked. I hadn't gone by that name since I was nineteen. A name only my mother uttered when she was angry at me. "It *is* you," the woman said, as we stood face to face. "You haven't changed a bit."

"Rosenda?" I asked hesitantly. "Rosenda Cabral."

She had short, permed hair now, and her complexion was clear. Heavier than the last time I'd seen her, she sported a yellow gold silk tee under a light brown jacket and pants.

"Mendoza, now," she quickly interjected. "I haven't seen you since . . ." She paused. In her gaze I could see joy and pain follow one another in sequence, like clouds and sunlight during a spring shower.

Her teary face stared at me from a corner of my memory, as she told me and my best friend Luisa, who would later be killed in the Cisneros investigation, that she was pregnant and would have to quit college. The three of us had grown up in Jingletown, a small residential area west of the Fruitvale District, surrounded on all sides now by industrial warehouses. The three of us had graduated from Fremont High School. But Luisa and I had decided to attend Cal State at Hayward, while Rosenda had gone to UC Berkeley, hoping to attend law school after graduation. She'd been one of the students at Berkeley who had joined the 1969 Third World Student strike. Luisa and I had heard her painful confession in the evening following one of the most violent confrontations between the police and the students. Three days after the riot, Rosenda's parents sent her to Oxnard to stay with relatives. Luisa and I didn't see her or hear from her again.

I wasn't sure if this Rosenda Mendoza, standing poised and self-assured before me now, was trying to remember or to forget the circumstances surrounding our last meeting.

"It seems so long ago. The strike, the National Guard on campus," I said. I reached for her hand. "It's so good to see you, Rosenda."

She sighed, smiled and squeezed my hand. "I'd heard that you'd become a private detective. It sounds exciting." Her eyes lit up. "As you can see now, I'm a legal secretary—Lester Zamora's." I sensed no regret in her eyes or her voice. "Mrs. Cartier told me that you want to see him."

"I'm working on a case that might have something to do with a former client of his."

"Is it urgent?"

"It is," I answered. "Literally a matter of life or death."

She gave me an inquisitive look. "He's going to be tied up all afternoon. Why don't you write him a note? I'll make sure he gets it quickly." She handed me a pad and pencil she'd been holding. "While you do that, I'll get an envelope." Turning around, she headed towards the reception desk.

I stood there for an instant, staring at the blank page. Discarding the idea of writing a detailed account, I wrote:

Licia Lecuona is in danger. We need to talk. If you're interested, call me.

I enclosed my business card with the note. At the door, we hugged each other, then Rosenda asked, "Any way we can have dinner soon?"

"I was about to suggest it," I told her. "How about day after tomorrow—Wednesday night?"

She agreed with a nod.

"How about seven o'clock at La Ultima, that New-Mexican restaurant on MacArthur and Thirty-eighth Avenue?"

"Great. I'll be there."

Resisting my impulse to drive by Licia Lecuona's old Victorian on East Twenty-seventh Street, I went to the office, paid bills, and billed clients for services performed. I didn't particularly like doing paperwork, but it usually gave me a feeling of accomplishment. Besides, Justin and I needed the money.

By the time I got home, I had a message from Rosenda that Lester Zamora could see me at his home on Madera Court, in the Maxwell Park area, at seven. I tried to reach Justin in Los Angeles, but he wasn't in his hotel room. Since he was scheduled to call me at about the time I would be at Lester's house, I left a message asking him to phone me in the late evening instead.

I was about to sit down to read more on "previous lives"

when my mother called. Usually we followed an unwritten script: She asked about my health, my daughter Tania, my daily activities, and news about Justin. Then she told me about *her* health and daily concerns. But this time, she went straight to the point and asked me if I had heard from the San Francisco police regarding Black Widow.

"And what about that other woman—the one in black?" she asked. "I bet *she* can tell you a few things about what happened. Have they found her?"

"No, they haven't," I replied. "And I don't know where to even begin to look for her."

After telling my mother briefly about my encounters with the reporter Celia Howard and with Rosenda, I asked her if she believed in reincarnation.

"I believe . . . in the life after, that I'm going to be reunited with your dad when I die," she said. "But reincarnation? I don't think I would *want* to come back. One journey through this vale of tears is enough for me. Why do you ask?"

"Licia Lecuona—Black Widow—apparently believes in reincarnation."

"I bet you Black Widow believes she was someone important in a past life. Just like my *comadre* Nina Contreras."

"Your *comadre!* I didn't know Mrs. Contreras believed in reincarnation," I said, amazed.

Nina Contreras, who was ten years younger than my mother, had once gone to see a number of fortunetellers. She was convinced that her husband's philanderings were the reason she'd won increasingly larger amounts of money in the California lottery. She'd hoped that one of the soothsayers would predict precisely when her husband would next be unfaithful again, so she could purchase the winning ticket for millions.

"Does she still think that reincarnated souls will help her win the lottery?" I asked.

My mother chuckled. "No, I think Nina's given up on that scheme. You know something though? You could talk to her. She might be able to explain this mumbo-jumbo to you, or put you in touch with someone who can."

"That's an idea," I said. "So who does Mrs. Contreras think she was in a past life?"

"So far, she was the wife of a successful businessman in Spain three hundred years ago. She was also a nun who had an orphanage and was revered as a saint," my mother explained with a chuckle. Then, in a sad tone, she added, "My *comadre* is a very unhappy woman. She has devoted her life to five children—including my godson—who can't even remember her birthday on time, and to a husband who's put her through hell. All she wants is a second chance at happiness. Don't you think? I mean, if not now, in the next life. But at least she didn't kill my *compadre* José. Maybe this Black Widow wants another chance, too—to make up for taking her husband's life."

Perhaps my mother was right. Perhaps Licia wanted only a second chance to restore the order she had upset when she killed Peter. But for Mrs. Contreras, even another painful journey through this "vale of tears" seemed better than facing the nothingness she feared.

SEVEN
The Soul's Eternal Query

What will remain of me when I'm gone? I wondered as I drove past Mills College on my way to Lester Zamora's house that Monday evening. *A pile of teeth and bones? Yes. A bunch of genes that might conceivably go on forever? Possibly. But the oak, eucalyptus, and redwood trees on this campus will live longer than the memory of me,* I thought, as I drove up a foothill towards Madera Court.

A loneliness and uncertainty I had never experienced before took residence in my chest. By the time I parked across the street from the Zamora house, I had begun to wonder what would happen to my own soul after I died. But I didn't get an opportunity to ponder my question, for at that moment the front door opened. A young woman walked out, leaving the door open behind her. She got into a red Mustang, which stood parked in the driveway next to a dark green Volvo, and drove away.

A large undraped front window displayed a peaceful, warm environment inside. For someone looking out, I imagined that the window offered a spectacular view of the East Oakland and San Leandro hills and flatlands. Bordering the Fruitvale District— the barrio—Maxwell Park was a modest district with nice houses still reasonably priced.

I was certain Lester Zamora could afford a house in any upper-class neighborhood in Oakland. I wondered why he had chosen to live in Maxwell Park.

I walked up the front steps and, although the door was ajar, rang the bell and waited. I heard salsa music and the clatter of dishes. The smell of fried tortillas reached my nostrils. I wasn't sure whether the familiar smell, my soul's query, or my fear awakened in me a sudden need to be held, but I fought off the feeling.

Stepping inside the door, I said, at the top of my lungs, "Hello? Mr. Zamora? Gloria Damasco here."

"*Pásale. Siéntate,*" a man's voice answered, using the familiar rather than formal verb forms: Come in and sit down.

The living room was decorated in the increasingly fashionable Santa Fe style, with an adobe fireplace, Navajo rugs on the floor, and large hand-painted ceramic pots. Paintings by Gorman and other popular Native American artists decorated the walls.

I could also see the dining room: The table had been set for three people, but one of the place settings had already been used. Perhaps the young woman I'd just seen leaving had already had her dinner.

On a long glass-top cedar coffee table in the living room, I saw some art books and a photo album. The album caught my attention immediately. On its smooth kidskin cover, a cactus flower and the name *Xochitl* had been engraved in delicate gold leaf. I sat down on the sofa and opened the album.

A photo of a newborn infant, asleep in someone's arms, gave my heart a slight jolt, as I remembered a similar baby photo of my daughter Tania in Darío's arms. I also couldn't help thinking about Licia Lecuona and how hard it must have been to lose her baby. I suddenly realized that Celia Howard hadn't mentioned the baby's sex and I had not asked about it at the time. Regardless, if Licia's baby had lived, he or she would be about Xochitl's age— if that was the girl I had seen drive away.

Trying to keep my mind off Black Widow's tragedy, if only for a few more minutes, I continued my perusal. Photos of all of the milestones in Xochitl's life were there. But some photos had apparently been removed, and her *quinceañera* and high-school graduation photos showed her with only her father. There were no photos of Xochitl with her mother.

In the last two photos, Xochitl appeared as she had looked leaving the house when I arrived. She had the same oval face and brown skin as her father and his straight hair. But, unlike his, her eyes were soulful and her smile barely a grin.

The music stopped and the swinging door opened. Wearing a

pullover sweater, brown pants, and sandals, Lester Zamora walked into the dining room, carrying a tray. He set it on the table and picked up a coffee mug from it. He took a sip as he approached me.

"*¿Bonita, no?*" he said when he saw the album opened to the last page.

"Yes. She is beautiful," I replied. "How old is Xochitl now?"

Beaming with delight, he answered, "She's eighteen. Just graduated last June. She's now at Mills College, just down the road."

"Congratulations," I said. "Mrs. Zamora and you have every reason to be proud of her."

His face turned somber. "Xochitl's mother left us sometime ago. But I'm sure she's also proud of her."

So "Xochitl's mother" hadn't died. Since there were no photos of her anywhere, I assumed she had been quietly deleted from the family history.

Lester began walking towards the dining room, and my attention quickly shifted back to him. He signaled for me to follow.

Out of habit, more than curiosity, I looked at a large number of recognition certificates and plaques on a wall. They had been awarded to him by a diverse number of Spanish-speaking and other organizations in the Bay Area.

"My trophies," he said. "*¿Quieres algo de comer o tomar?*" He pointed at the food tray.

"It all looks good," I said, as I surveyed the *flautas*, *guacamole*, and salad on the tray. "I hope you don't mind, but I'll pass. I'll have a glass of mineral water, though, if you have any," I said.

"No drinking or eating on the job, eh?" he remarked as he walked towards the bar refrigerator.

"Something like that," I replied.

If my presence made him uneasy in any way, he didn't show it. On the other hand, at five-feet-four, one-hundred twenty pounds, I hardly represented any threat to a man at least five inches taller and fifty pounds heavier than me.

"I hope you don't mind if I eat while we talk. I didn't have lunch and, frankly, I'm starved," he explained, as he handed me a glass. "So, tell me. What makes you think that Licia is in danger?" he asked between mouthfuls.

I summarized the events I had witnessed during and after the Procession of the Dead in San Francisco. He stopped eating and listened closely to every detail about the conquistador soldiers on horseback, the abduction of the woman in black, the weapon used on Licia, and the acrobat's stunt. I then related my conversation with the San Francisco police and my futile efforts to locate Licia or the woman in black. He decided to finish his meal as I related my conversation with Celia Howard. But he pushed his plate away when I began talking about Licia's diary and the death of her baby.

His countenance showed me that Licia's tragedy still affected him deeply. But I wasn't sure whether he felt anger, remorse, or resentment. I left out any mention of Licia's belief in reincarnation and her hiring of a private detective.

"So, do you think there is a connection between Peter Lecuona's . . . death, and what's happening to Licia now?" he asked.

"Not necessarily," I answered. "But since I don't know anything about her life in prison, that's all I have to work with. I was hoping you would be able to fill in the gaps."

He tensed up, then gave me a hard look, but he remained quiet. His look made me feel even more unsettled, but I held his gaze. I had my hand wrapped around the glass of cold water and I suddenly became aware of the numbness in my fingers. I eased my grip and gradually let go of the glass, without taking my eyes off him.

"I'll make a deal with you," he finally said. "You tell me your client's name and I'll tell you what I know. *Tú sabes*, I'm not going to tell you anything that Licia told me in confidence as her lawyer." He pushed his chair away from the table, sat back in it, and crossed his legs.

Time for a showdown, I thought. My hands felt colder than ever. But I looked him in the eye as I said, "I'm not working for anyone. I have no client."

"I see. You're just a concerned citizen."

"I'm sorry to have bothered you," I said, pushing my chair back. "I was under the impression that you cared for Licia. My mistake." I began to get up.

He straightened up in his chair and smiled. "Okay. Relax. *Siéntate. Vamos a hablar.*" He got up, went to the bar, and helped himself to some brandy. "Let's start by being honest. You're a private detective and I'm a lawyer. We deal in facts. Or we *should*, anyway. My gut tells me that you're not being straightforward with me. Am I wrong?"

I wasn't about to tell him my client's name, but there was something else at work in me. I fought my desire to tell him. I asked myself if I really trusted this man, a stranger, enough to confide in him.

As if sensing my thoughts, he commanded, "Try me."

"I have a dark gift. I see things that other people can't see," I told him. I was amazed at how easily the words poured out.

"I see," he said. Then, with a smile, he added, "No pun intended. "You're *clairvoyant*? Is that what you're trying to tell me?"

"I am. For better or worse."

"I was raised by my mother and two aunts. Did you know that?"

I shook my head.

"My mother died a long time ago, but I'm still very close to my aunts. They're both very old now. They live in Salinas. When I visit them, my aunt Sofía who, unlike me, is light-skinned and has green eyes, proudly tells me that we haven't a drop of *Indian* blood in us. Then she proceeds to tell me all about the extra-terrestrial beings who are coming to take all the members of our family—one of the chosen families—to another planet, for the earth is *doomed to perish soon*.

"But my aunt Clara . . . well, she's something else," Lester continued. "She's practical, straightforward, and doesn't have an ounce of prejudice in her heart. Over the years, whenever I've gone to see her, Aunt Clara has always told me what she sees in store for me. She's been right many times. So, you see, you don't have to convince me that people with dark gifts exist." He was quiet for a moment. "What do you see in store for Licia?"

"My gift is not as great as your aunt's. The things I see are rather cryptic and they come to me in dreams at first," I said, then told him about my dream. "I know her baby died, but, in my dream, she has a daughter and a son. Her son kills her."

Suddenly, Lester Zamora turned his gaze away from me. "I see what you mean by cryptic." When he reached for his glass, I detected a slight tremor of his hand. "Then, your dream must have a different meaning." He sipped his brandy.

"There's always that possibility. I won't know until the other visions come," I said. "Given the attempt on Licia's life, I don't dare dismiss anything as not important."

"But this place you see in your dream seems so unusual. Do you have any idea where it is?"

"Not a clue . . . yet, but it might be where she's living now. Do you know where she is?"

"In her house on East Twenty-seventh. It's not at all like the place you describe. I haven't seen her since her release. I suppose she wants to start a new life," he said and sighed.

"Did you ever visit Licia in prison?"

"Oh, yes. Many times. She had no one left but me. I couldn't abandon her, not even after my wife asked me to stop going to see her. Helena had no reason to be jealous, but she was, of Licia. I suppose I can't blame Helena for leaving. I broke every promise I ever made to her. And now Licia doesn't want anything to do with me. Isn't it ironic?"

When he realized all he'd said, his face turned red, and his upper lip twitched slightly.

"I'm sorry. I didn't mean to imply that Licia's responsible for my divorce. Helena and I did that. It was very difficult for my wife to understand my relationship with Licia."

"It's always difficult for husband and wife to understand and accept each other's special relationships," I offered.

He nodded.

We were both quiet for a moment, Lester in his sorrows, and I trying to find a tactful way back to the subject.

"Did Licia ever talk to you about anything that happened to her in prison? Do you know if she became close to anyone there? Or if anyone had anything against her?" I finally asked.

He looked at me with unfocused eyes. I repeated my questions. Pushing his shoulders back, he attempted a smile. "There was someone in prison Licia felt very close to for the last three years. This woman—I think her name is Rosa—was also an inmate there. She became some sort of spiritual guide for her."

"What was Rosa in for?"

"She was smuggling hallucinogenics over the border—mostly mushrooms and mescaline. Licia said that Rosa used the drugs only for religious purposes."

"Do you believe that?"

He shrugged. "Licia believed it."

"Is this Rosa still in prison? I'd like to have a talk with her."

"I don't know where the woman is now. But I do know some people in the Department of Corrections. I'll try to find out her whereabouts if you think it's important."

"I'd sure appreciate that," I said. "By the way, I understand that Licia hired a private investigator to do some work for her while she was in prison. Do you know what that was about?"

"Who told you that?" He was trying to sound casual, but his quivering upper lip told a different story.

This time, I let silence do my work for me.

Lester played with his glass for a while, then finally said, "I have no idea why Licia hired a private detective. Is it important?" he asked. He knew about Dora Saldaña.

"It probably isn't," I said. "I appreciate your seeing me." I got up and pushed the chair gently under the table.

"No problem," he said. "I count on your keeping all this to yourself—especially what I told you about my aunt Clara," he requested. "Clients and fellow attorneys tend not to trust anyone who delves into the *occult*, quote unquote."

He reeled back a little as he got up. I looked at the glass of brandy half-full on the table. Yet I suspected it wasn't alcohol that made him stagger as he walked me to the door.

As I drove off, I thought of Lester surrounded by all his awards and diplomas. I remembered something Mami Julia was fond of saying: Human beings don't go to their graves wondering why they didn't accomplish this or that. On their deathbeds, they regret not having expressed their love for someone clearly and often.

I wondered what name Lester Zamora's regret bore: Helena, or Licia?

EIGHT
Shadows in the Attic

I left the Zamora house looking forward to a soak in the tub, a glass of merlot by the fire, and a long-distance talk with Justin. But as I got off the MacArthur Freeway, I followed an impulse and turned left on Beaumont towards Highland Hospital. With its long front staircase and twin tower architecture, the old building resembled a church or castle more than a hospital.

Built in 1926 to minister to indigent folk, the county health facility had once been one of the most modern and complete hospitals in the country. Highland Hospital had long ago stopped enjoying such a fine reputation. Still, there was always a great deal of activity at its emergency room.

Trying to avoid the two shrieking ambulances approaching fast from both ends of Fourteenth Avenue, I circled around to East Twenty-seventh Street.

I slowed down as soon as I saw Licia's house. It was dark and seemed uninhabited. Yet, even dimly illuminated by the street light, the grounds looked well cared for. The iron fence and the locked gate had been recently painted.

As I looked up at the attic, I thought I saw a silhouette move across the window. Soon after, I realized it was only the shadow cast by the swaying branches of the eucalyptus trees next to the house. But something was going on in the house next door. Two dogs were barking furiously, despite their owner's warning. I backed up and parked across the street from the Victorian as a burglar alarm went off, drowning for an instant all other noise.

I was getting ready to get out of my car when a leashed pit-bull and hound, with their master on tow, tore out of the house. The dogs barked and tugged with such vigor that their owner, a heavy and tall white man as fierce-looking as his dogs, had a hard time controlling them.

Suddenly, the dogs were silent. The hound stood on its hind legs and sniffed the air; the pit-bull scratched the iron gate. A tall woman came out of the man's house, climbed on one of the two motorcycles in their driveway, wheeled it out and parked it at the curb. She stayed with it. The man looked in my direction. It was too late for me to hide, so I decided to get out of the car.

"What's going on?" I inquired, staying close to my car.

"Who're you?" he asked.

The dogs growled. The man gave a little slack to their leashes. I stood in place, taking deep breaths to slow down the beating of my heart. When he was sure I intended no harm, he patted the dogs' heads. They sat on their haunches with their eyes still fixed on me.

"I was coming to see the people in that house," I said. Not wanting to upset the dogs, I raised my arm slowly to point at Licia's house.

"They're not home," he said. "But someone else is. Two guys. Jumped over my fence. Chaka and Cleo here were chained." He tapped their heads respectively as he said their names. "Otherwise they would've made mincemeat of them."

"I have a cell phone. Would you like me to call the police?"

"No need," he replied. "My old lady already called."

Chaka and Cleo began to growl again and became quite restless. Pulling on their leashes, the man said, "Here they come."

I expected to see an OPD patrol. Instead, I saw a burgundy Buick come up the hill, a man at the wheel. It slowed down as it approached the house. The gate began to open as the neighbor waved at the driver. I got back in my car but kept the window down.

The Buick's driver lowered his window and spoke briefly with the neighbor. Privacy glass on the rear windows allowed only a glimpse of two shadows.

The Buick went a short way up the driveway and parked. The riders stayed inside the vehicle. Then I noticed a second car, a dark

Taurus, coming up the street with a woman at the wheel. It sped up past the house. I watched the car in my side mirror as it parked a discreet distance away. I waited for the driver to get out, but she didn't. Since neighbors had begun to gather on both sidewalks, I wondered if she was just another curious passerby.

Less than a minute later, an OPD patrol drove up and parked. The police officer was just getting out of the car when a second patrol car approached from the opposite direction.

"There they go! They're getting away!" one of the neighbors shouted abruptly.

I saw the silhouettes of two people running towards the fence at the end of the yard. The next-door neighbor unleashed his dogs, who took off in pursuit of the shadows, but the intruders had already scaled the fence.

The second patrol took off down the street towards the hospital. The man called his dogs, commanding them to run in the opposite direction. He climbed on his motorcycle and rode after them. I got out of the car. Since the police had everything under control, I decided to keep an eye on the Taurus, still parked up the street, and the Buick.

I turned my attention to the remaining policeman, who was talking to the driver of the Buick. A moment later, the driver got out. He and the officer walked towards the front door and went inside. The alarm stopped blaring, but both men remained in the house. Lights went on in sequence, first on the ground floor, then the second, and finally the attic.

"It looks beau-ti-ful! Like in the old times, when Miss Roman was alive," said a woman behind me. I turned to look at her. She was about seventy years old, leaning on a younger man's arm.

"Did you know Gabriela Román?" I asked. I took a few steps back until I was alongside her.

"Oh, yes," the old woman answered. "Bless her soul. She was a very nice person. Generous. Did you know she helped me buy my little house here?" she asked. "I was a widow, you see, with three young children, living in a shack. I did laundry for Miss Roman and for Miss Hollister, the school teacher who then lived in this little house—my house. She died and her relatives were selling the house, and I had lost that job. My Jimmy died of consumption, you see. But I say 'twas the heat in that steel mill that dried up his lungs. The Devil's cauldron."

The younger man smiled at me and shook his head. "Momma, I'm sure this lady's got better things to do than listen to old tales 'bout Miss Roman."

"It's okay," I reassured her. "I'm interested."

"Miss Roman said, 'You know, Jimmy's pension is not enough to raise your children. Come work for me. I'll pay you fifty dollars a week and I'll help you buy that little house across the street, so you can keep an eye on your young ones, too.' She being a widow, see, she understood. Imagine anyone being so generous now. And she made good on all of her promises. She did. I worked for her twenty years, 'til she passed away."

"It must have been very hard when her son and daughter-in-law died," I said.

"Oh, so you know the family," the old woman said. "A terrible thing. But having her granddaughter to look after made Miss Roman real happy. Lishie, she was so quiet, so grownup, no trouble for Miss Roman. But Miss Roman couldn't see the child wasn't well. Sad. She was a sad child. I was glad Miss Roman wasn't here no more when that evil man moved into her house. Evil, that man was evil as they come."

I assumed she was talking about Peter Lecuona. "Yes, he was. A terrible tragedy."

"Poor Lishie. They shoulda pinned a medal on her, not sent her to that Godforsaken place."

"At first, no one wanted to live in that house. I guess on account of the murder," the son said. "But with all those looneys from the hospital, things got jumpin' round 'ere for awhile. Then that no good drug kingpin moved in. He did business there for two years. Dealers in and out of that house at all hours. Then one day he got what he deserved, gunned down, right by the hospital, with three cops standing there talking and having their coffee by the Quick Stop. Then all of them druggies and looneys start-

ed coming back, breaking into the house. I guess they were looking for the kingpin's stash. That's when me and the neighbors
decided to organize. We'd had enough."

"Yes," the old woman interjected. "We went to talk to the
landlord and told him about it. He didn't even know what was
going on. He said he was going to send some security people to
live there and install an alarm. And he did."

The cop and the driver of the Buick came out of the house.
The driver got in the car and drove up the driveway. The automatic door lifted and the car disappeared into the darkness of the
garage.

The officer came down to the curb and told everyone to go
home. The second patrol pulled up. The cops stood on the street,
exchanging notes, then got in their respective cars and left. A few
seconds later, the dogs returned from up the street, led by their
master on his motorcycle.

The woman's son went to talk to his neighbor, who was pet-
ting his dogs. He came back shortly. "They didn't catch 'em
hoodlums." Turning to his mother, he said, "Let's go in,
Momma." To me, he said, "Goodnight."

The Taurus was still parked on the same spot. Trying not to
arouse further suspicion, I decided to drive down to the corner
and make a U-turn. When I got back to the spot, the Taurus was
gone. I headed home.

I had barely walked into my house, when the phone rang. I
was happy to hear Justin's voice.

"How's it going?" I asked. I hoped that he would say he was
coming back soon.

"Not good," he said, exasperated. "I'm afraid I won't be able
to get back to the Bay Area for a while. How are you doing?"

I brought him up to date.

"It sounds like drugs might be involved."

"It might be a coincidence. It's difficult to tell at this time. But
I can't find out what it's all about unless I get closer to Licia
Lecuona."

"Why don't you talk to Michael about it? He might be able to arrange a meeting."

"I've thought about that, but Michael is out of town until Thursday. In the meantime, I'd like to have a talk with Dora Saldaña, the Ace investigator, and with Rosa, Licia's former prison mate."

Justin agreed. He gave me the phone number where he could be reached. "I'll call you tomorrow, about this time." He paused. "Be careful. Back off if it doesn't look good. Better to live with regret and haunted by visions than not at all."

For a moment, I flirted with the idea of telling him I was in love with him. But I fought off the temptation. It wasn't the time yet.

After I hung up, I had no trouble talking myself out of reading any more about previous lives. Instead, I sat on the loveseat in the living room with only the glow and warmth of the fire around me, thinking about Licia. I knew many facts about her, mostly gathered from other people's accounts. But I had no more idea who Licia—or Black Widow, for that matter—was than I did that first time I saw her on the Day of the Dead, carrying marigolds and the photo of the husband she had murdered.

NINE
The Menacing Hand

Down a dark tunnel, I run after someone, but I can't tell who. A man's hand emerges from the darkness, the long, thin fingers and thumb wrapped around the stock of a pistol. An elegant hand. How can such a beautiful hand, more suited for the piano or the guitar, wield an instrument of death?. The hand retreats back into the darkness. "Why did you take him from me?" questions a raspy voice—I cannot tell if man or woman.

Suddenly I am pursuing the acrobat up a long staircase. A sharp pain stabs at my belly. I fall on my knees, gasping for breath.

Bathed in perspiration, the left side of my abdomen on fire, I woke up. I sat up in bed and caught a glimpse of myself in the dresser mirror: a middle-aged woman, pale and drawn, as if only part of her soul remained in her body. I turned away and pulled the covers over my head, lying in bed very still, trying to hear the beating of my heart, trying not to think of my dream, until I fell asleep again.

The bleak November sun was already high in the sky when I looked at the clock-radio next to my bed. It was ten in the morning. I had slept ten hours, yet I felt exhausted. I would have preferred to stay in bed all day, but the prospect of going over and over my dreams, trying to find their connection to the attempts on Licia's life, was drearier than going through the day with only half my soul in me.

When I got to the office, I had a message waiting from Rosenda, my childhood friend and Lester Zamora's secretary: Rosa Catalino was the name of Licia's "spiritual guide" in prison. She had been released from prison the year before, and her last known address was on East Fourteenth Street in the Fruitvale District.

Since Rosa Catalino had made her living as a "spiritual guide," I decided to consult in the Yellow Pages. Between Prosthetic Devices and Psychiatrists, I found her. "*Soy la mejor consejera de almas*," wrote Sister Rosa about herself. I am the best of spiritual counselors. The address Lester had given me for Rosa Catalino was the same as that for "Sister Rosa." I jotted down the telephone number.

I decided to ask my mother's friend, Nina Contreras, to go with me for a consultation. My mother offered to call Nina and ask her to make an appointment with Sister Rosa on my behalf.

"I'm sure she'll be delighted," my mother said. "She'll probably want to go *with* you. When do you want to see this Sister Rosa?"

"Today, if possible. Maybe late afternoon, early evening."

"What do you want Nina to say?"

"I'm her niece and in dire need of spiritual guidance. I'm interested in past-life regressions."

"How much are you willing to pay? As I understand from Nina, it can be quite expensive. You know, Nina has spent most of her lottery winnings going to these *espiritistas*."

"Up to fifty dollars an hour, no more—and hopefully a lot less." I was going to have a hard time justifying the expense to Michael Cisneros.

I verified the address I had for Ace Security and Investigations in San Leandro, a city south of Oakland. The traffic was even slower than usual on the MacArthur Freeway, but fifteen minutes later, I arrived outside the ASI offices, which were protected by a surveillance camera and an electronically controlled iron gate. The camera focused on me as soon as I picked up the phone next to the gate. A man's husky voice told me to state my name and business.

"My name is Gloria Vélez," I said, using my maiden name. "I'd like to speak to Dora Saldaña."

Static followed my request. The man said something I

couldn't quite understand. The *click* that followed his grunts was a sure sign that my request had been denied. After standing there for about five minutes, under the scrutiny of the electronic eye, I rang the bell again. A minute later, the man with the husky voice opened the door and stepped onto the patio.

"What's your business with Dora Saldaña?" he asked.

"I'd like to talk to her about an old client of hers," I answered.

"What's the client's name?" he asked, eyeing me with suspicion.

"Mine. I am the client," I said and stared back at him.

Taken aback by my answer, he said, "It doesn't matter who you are. Ms. Saldaña doesn't work here anymore." I could sense his irritation in the way he said her name.

"Do you know how I can get in touch with her?"

"I fired her about six months ago."

"Why did you that? What did she do?"

"She was a disloyal, unreliable employee, with an attitude," he told me. Then, in a softer tone, he added, "But if you're in need of assistance, maybe we can help."

"My problem *is* finding her," I said. "I gave her five hundred dollars last year to follow my husband. I never heard from her again. I need that money. I want it back, but I can't find her. Her phone is disconnected, and I don't know where she lives." Then, as sweetly as I could manage, I asked, "How about giving me her last-known address?"

"No use looking for her there. She moved. Disappeared into thin air," he answered and snapped his fingers.

"Did she also take your money?" I asked.

His face turned red. "No, not money. Something more valuable. She took some of our clients with her when she left. I didn't know she was doing outside work for some of our clients. She knew that no one, *no one*, is allowed to go solo at ASI." He emphasized his anger by hitting the gate with the butt of his hand. "Now, do me a favor. Here's my card. If you find that . . . that witch, let me know. I'd like to have a *little talk* with her myself."

"Sure thing."

"Hey," he said, "give me a call if you still want your husband followed, or anything else." He winked at me.

"As soon as I get my money back," I chirped as I left.

As I walked down the street towards my car, I had the strong feeling that someone was watching me. I turned around, but the ASI man had already gone back into his office. Remembering the black Ford Taurus parked outside Licia's house the night before, I looked around, but I didn't spot any car like it.

Who could be following me and why, I wondered, as I got in my car. The only people I had told about the attempt on Licia's life were the writer Celia Howard and attorney Lester Zamora. I could find no reason for Celia to follow me or have me followed. On the other hand, although Lester had been friendly and somewhat helpful to me, he hadn't been completely honest with me. For some unexplained reason, I remembered the fragments of my dream that morning. I focused on the voice I'd heard. Who had taken whom away? There was some connection between what had happened at the Zamora house and what I had heard in my vision; at the moment, it eluded me.

The cell phone buzzed. Before I could say hello, my mother informed me that Nina and I had an appointment with "Sister Rosa" at six o'clock.

"Perfect. That'll give me enough time to make a quick trip to UC Berkeley."

"What's in Berkeley?"

"That's where Professor Legorreta, Peter Lecuona's brother-in-law, teaches," I explained. "Please tell Nina I'll pick her up at five-thirty. Thanks, Mom."

"Gloria Inés, *why* are you getting involved in this mess? It might be getting time you find out, before you go any further."

"I will, Mom," I assured her. In fact, I now believed I had no choice but to follow through with my investigation. Not only did I have a paying client, I was also certain that if Licia were killed because of my apathy or fear, I would not be able to forgive myself.

TEN
The Red Side of Retribution

On my way to Cal-Berkeley, I had a craving for a *taco de carne asada* and made a quick stop at a *taquería* on University Avenue. I usually didn't eat a lot of chile peppers. But they looked so inviting, I had more than a generous serving.

As I bit into a jalapeño, I felt my heart beat with renewed fervor. I doubted any part of my soul was still at large. Afer patting the sweat off my forehead and upper lip with a napkin, I sprinkled some salt on the back of my hand and licked it, then drank a glass of iced water to alleviate the burning sensation on my tongue. This was Mami Julia's remedy for the sting of a hot pepper. It worked.

I drove to Bancroft Way. After I parked in the student union underground garage, I walked up Bancroft Way towards Kroeber Hall, where the anthropology department and museum were housed.

I had not been to the Berkeley campus in many years. It was a pleasant walk, and I enjoyed seeing more Latino, African-American and Asian faces in the large crowd of students rushing to and from the campus or milling around the cafes and shops at the corner of Bancroft Way and Telegraph Avenue. It hadn't been so back in 1969 during the Third World Student Strike on campus. At the time, a small group of students had demanded that Cal-Berkeley make an effort to recruit more minority students.

During the six-month strike, students from Cal-State Hayward and junior colleges in the area, including my poet friend Luisa Cortez and me, had joined Rosenda Cabral and others in the picket lines right at that corner, then at Sather Gate. We had been there also when, under the mutual aid policy, Alameda

County Sheriff's deputies and California highway patrolmen had joined city and campus police officers to quash the student insurrection. It all had ended in a violent confrontation and the subsequent deployment of the National Guard to Berkeley. Lost in my memories, I went up to the reception desk and waited quietly. The receptionist was on the phone for quite a while, speaking in whispers and occasional giggles. Eventually I cleared my throat to announce my presence, but she ignored me. Two other calls interrupted her *tête-à-tête*, but she put them on hold.

When she was through with her conversation, she picked up the other lines one by one and became irate with the callers who, tired of waiting, had hung up. Looking at the bookbag next to her desk, I concluded that the young, long-haired brunette was a student worker.

She finally turned her attention to me: "Can I help you?"

"I wonder if I may see Professor Legorreta," I said, as politely as possible.

"He's not in," she replied. The phone rang again and I closed my eyes in an effort to remain calm.

"Any idea what time Professor Legorreta will be back?" I asked after she hung up.

"Try again in August," she said with a smirk. "He's on sabbatical this year."

The exhilarating effect of the chile peppers on my soul was evaporating rapidly. "Is it possible to get his phone number at home? It's very important that I get in touch with him."

"No way, José! We're not allowed to give out anyone's phone numbers or addresses, including mine," she said as she opened a desk drawer. Retrieving her handbag, she pulled a hairbrush from it. "Mind if I ask you a question?" she asked nonchalantly while she brushed her hair. Her voice became softer, even a bit mellifluous. "Are you Reuben Rodriguez's mother?"

"No. But I'm his aunt," I said, lying through my teeth but sounding matter-of-fact. "How did you know Reuben and I are related?"

"He looks a lot like you, and your being an older woman and a Shicana . . . Well, I thought maybe you were his mother."

"I see. He's handsome, isn't he?"

"Uh-huuh!" she exclaimed.

With a sweet voice, I pleaded for Professor Legorreta's number once again.

"I really can't," the young woman said, "I can lose my job and I need it."

"I wouldn't want you to lose your job," I said. Perhaps I could get her to talk to Rafael Escobar, Justin's cousin, who was applying to Berkeley. Rafael had done odd jobs for Justin and me.

"You know," I said, "my son, Rafael, Reuben's cousin, is applying to Cal. He's going to be majoring in anthropology. That's why I wanted to talk to Professor Legorreta. Are you majoring in anthropology too?"

When she answered with a nod, I asked her if she might talk to Rafael, to give him some idea about courses he should take and other important matters. "And he can tell you everything you want to know about Reuben," I added.

"Really?" she remarked. "I'd love to meet Rafael. Tell him to call me . . . better yet, to come and see me. I'm here from one to four every afternoon." She scribbled her name and number on a paper.

I threw a quick glance at the slip of paper then at the office clock. It was three forty-five. By the time I got hold of Rafael, "Melissa" would be gone. "He'll probably call you tomorrow, Melissa."

"Cool," the young woman said.

Outside the office, I searched in my handbag for my cell phone. Rafael's line was busy. After a few more unsuccessful attempts, I started back to Oakland. I stopped at an ATM and withdrew some cash to pay "Sister Rosa."

At home, planning how to broach with Rosa the subject of her relationship with Licia, I looked over the notes I'd taken while reading about reincarnation. I came across something I'd copied:

Karma is cause and effect, red and green. Also called the Law of Retribution, its causes and effects can be traced back to the actions of previous selves in past lives. When we gain the knowledge of who we have been and what we have done, change can be effected in our present life. Then, retribution becomes not a negative force—red—but a positive one—green.

"Retribution," I said aloud. I went over my list of people with possible motives to seek retribution from Licia. I had no idea what the Lecuona family might have been up to, but they remained on my short list of suspects. Unless my intuition was totally off target, after meeting Lester Zamora the night before, I had already made up my mind that he wasn't the one trying to kill Licia Lecuona. But what if someone indirectly but gravely affected by Licia's actions was involved? Someone related to the Lecuonas or, perhaps, someone connected with Lester?

"Helena Zamora, Lester's ex-wife," I said under my breath. Perhaps hers was the voice in my dream. *Why did you take him from me?* It made sense. I felt my heart pick up its pace.

From what Lester had blurted out the night before, Helena had been jealous of Licia for some time. His devotion to Licia had been the reason his wife had finally left him and their daughter. For Helena, the green side of karma had turned red. Perhaps she hadn't been able to do anything about it because Licia was behind bars. But now, Licia was out.

Where was Helena Zamora now, I wondered as I drove down the MacArthur Freeway for the fifth consecutive time that day. I felt like a modern Sisyphus, going nowhere but back and forth on a road full of bumps, detours, and dead-ends.

When I arrived at Mrs. Contreras's house on Seminary Avenue, she was waiting for me at the door. Since we had a good half hour before our appointment with Rosa Catalino, I decided to drive down city streets if only to change the scenery.

Mrs. Contreras asked me if I had ever consulted a spiritualist. She proceeded to tell me what I should expect. Most likely, there would be icons and religious images everywhere, pictures of spiritual guides and gurus, amulets, utensils and instruments used in magic rituals, tapestries, dusty books, and stacks of magazines and old newspapers.

"Don't expect anything to be clean. I guess the spirits don't care if a place is kept up or not."

"That's not a problem," I said. "But tell me about the session itself."

"Sister Rosa will probably talk with you for a while. She'll want to know what kind of problems you have or why you're seeking her help. She'll probably explain what she's going to do, then have you do some breathing exercises to relax you. Finally, she's going to put you under."

"Put me *under?*"

"Make you go deeper into your subconscious, like in a hypnotic trance," Mrs. Contreras said.

I looked at her. She must have seen the apprehension in my eyes, because she patted my hand. "Don't worry about it. It isn't like they really hypnotize you, and then you go kill someone. You're aware of everything that goes on around you."

She searched in her handbag and pulled out a microcassette tape recorder. "Just to make sure they're not going to mess around with my mind, I always ask if I can tape the session. If this Sister Rosa doesn't let us tape the session, we walk."

I laughed. "You're pretty smart. You should be the detective."

"No way. Many years ago, I followed my José to see if he was seeing a floozie at María's Beauty Shop on Fruitvale Avenue. He spotted me right away," Nina said, laughing. "I got so nervous, trying to get away, that I knocked over the garbage cans in front of the beauty shop. The floozie had to come out and clean up the mess. *That* made me feel good." She scratched her head, then added, "You probably think I'm like a teenager, a middle-aged adolescent."

"Desperate situations require desperate remedies. I'm sure you have your reasons. Besides, in love and war everything is permissible. But do me a favor. Next time, wear a wig and dark glasses. And use someone else's car."

Nina Contreras laughed. "Better yet, I'll hire you to tail him." She paused. "It must be very exciting to be a private detective." "Sometimes it is. Most of the time, it feels like any other job. Still, I love doing what I do."

"I know what you mean. I love making lace, but, some days, I look at my rough, stiff hands, and my fingers all bent out of shape. And for what, I ask myself. I begin to see *mi oficio como una maldición*—a curse for whatever sins I've committed in some past life," she said, stretching her hands out so I could see them. "For weeks I don't make lace. I clean the house from top to bottom. I bake bread. I do my gardening. But my bones get cold, and I feel every little pain in my joints. My mind wanders. And I begin to feel useless and old. In time, I go back to my lace. Then, I feel good again. Can you believe it?"

"I can," I replied. "Many artists feel that way."

"Artist," she exclaimed, then leaned forward, her eyes seeking mine. "I'm not an artist."

I met her gaze and smiled. "You are, Mrs. Contreras. Believe me. You have the soul of an artist." I remembered the beautiful christening gown Nina had made for Tania. "Have you ever thought of selling your lace to make some money?"

"I tried once, and I made some money. But José got very angry. *Do you want to embarrass me in front of my friends?*" she mimicked. "*Now they're going to say that I'm not man enough to support my family.*"

I looked briefly at Nina. She gave me a wide smile, but I could see tears in her eyes. "Pita's lucky to have a daughter like you," she said, then laid her head back on the seat rest.

ELEVEN
La zorra

A young woman opened the door of Sister Rosa's house and showed us to a sparsely furnished room. She asked us to wait there for Sister Rosa. Two wooden chairs and two armchairs encircled a round table. An afghan lay over a settee with small lace-covered pillows on it. I looked around for the stacks of dusty magazines or newspapers, but there weren't any. The room was spotless and cool. The only color and light were provided by six large Mexican beeswax candles with pink and blue paraffin roses around their bases.

On a large table in a corner, I saw American Indian drums of various sizes, a corncob pipe, a black Oaxacan incense burner with white ash in it, a box of kitchen matches, and next to it a large crystal jar filled with leaves.

"Sage," Mrs. Contreras said, picking up the jar and sniffing. Then, she went to inspect the lace pillowcovers. "Machine-made," she informed me. Looking at the bare walls, she remarked, "I'm sure this is the waiting room, not the consultation room."

A door opened. A short, dark-skinned woman stepped into the room, staying close to the door. She wore a long, loose, black, Mexican cotton dress with flowers embroidered on its long sleeves. Her black hair was braided and wrapped around her head, making her face seem rounder. She bowed her head slightly, then, without waiting for our greeting, walked to the corner table, took four sage leaves from the jar, dropped them into the incense burner, struck a match, and lit them.

As plumes of blue smoke rose from the burner, I tried to get a sense of her, but I couldn't. I felt as if a swirling barrier of light surrounded her, and I was unable to get through it. Not knowing why, I felt uneasy. I had to keep reminding myself that I was there to get some answers about Licia Lecuona.

She looked directly into my eyes. "Please, join me. First, we must invoke the spirits that rule your life."

Holding the burner in both hands, she walked to the center of the room. She signaled for me to stand behind her. Not knowing what to do, Mrs. Contreras stood aside. "You, too," Rosa said to her. Bright-eyed, Nina joined us.

Rosa raised the smoking burner. She spoke in a language that sounded vaguely familiar, but I couldn't quite make it out. Turning to our right four times, until we had completed a full circle, she invoked the spirits. At that moment, I realized that she was speaking in Nahuatl, the language of the Aztecs, still spoken by some tribes in Mexico.

The ritual over, she pointed at the settee with her open hand. Propping the pillows up to support my back, I sat. With a similar gesture, she asked Mrs. Contreras to take one of the armchairs, and she sat down in the other. I had taken my shoes off, and my feet and legs were getting cold, so I pulled the afghan over them. I was still restless.

Mrs. Contreras took the recorder out of her bag, turned it on, and put it on the table. Rosa looked at it but said nothing. Mrs. Contreras smiled at me, proud of having done her duty.

Rosa rested her left arm on the table but raised her hand until its open palm was directed at me, then closed her eyes. She asked me to close mine, take three deep breaths, and concentrate on my breathing.

"We are one. I cannot harm you, nor you me," she said in Spanish. After that, she said something in Nahuatl, then spoke in English. "Two spirits inhabit you. The spirits of *el tecolote*—the owl, whose knowing eyes see in all directions—and of *la zorra*—the fox, a crafty hunter. Long ago, when your dual soul was new, you chose the night as your domain. Darkness surrounded you; inside you there was light. But one day, you grew tired of seeing small creatures stalked by the night hunters. You called to them, warning them of their impending deaths, but they ignored your cries. So you closed your eyes, your wings became stiff, and *tecolote* saw no more and flew no more. Now, *tecolote* leaves your body at night and you dream of things to come. The spirit of the crafty *zorra* in you stalks the hunters, waiting for the right time to steal their living prey. It is the *zorra* that has brought you to me."

My heart began to beat slower and slower as Rosa spoke. Her voice, rhythmic and incantational, kept my mind engaged. My eyes felt heavy. I wanted to open them, but I couldn't. I struggled to make my body move again, but it refused to obey. Suddenly, I felt as if I were climbing out of a dark hole. I stopped as I reached the opening. I was on the edge of a precipice. I saw far below an immense valley with many cities and towns scattered in its midst, like building blocks strewn around by a toddler's hand. One of those towns was my destination. I jumped over the edge and found myself in flight.

At that instant, I heard a voice say, "Bring her out of it. Bring her out. *Now*."

I struggled to remain airborne, but the voice had cut into my desire for flight. Soon, feeling every turn in my stomach, I was spiraling down at great speed, a bird struck senseless by a stone. Just as I was about to hit the ground, I opened my eyes and sat up, gasping for breath.

"It's okay," Nina said. She was sitting next to me, rubbing my hands. "You're not falling. You're safe, on the ground."

When Nina said that, I realized that I had been talking and gesturing all the time, even though I didn't remember doing it. My stomach felt upset, but my mind was clear. I looked at Rosa Catalino, who observed me quietly, with eyes wider but melancholic ever as.

"Why has *la zorra* come to see me?" she asked calmly.

I fought back the nausea. Fearing that I would not have another chance, I said, "It's about a friend of yours, Licia Lecuona."

For an instant, I thought I saw a glimmer of delight in her eyes. A half smile formed in her lips, but it quickly faded. "So this is all about Doña Marina."

"Not Marina . . ." Nina started to say, but she stopped when I squeezed her hand.

"Is that who she was? Who was Doña Marina?" I asked.

"So she hasn't told you," Rosa said. "You must not be that close a friend of hers."

Suddenly, I remembered that Celia Howard had mentioned Licia's prison request for some books on the history of Mexico. In Mexican history, Doña Marina, also known as La Malinche, was an Indian woman who had helped Hernán Cortés, the Spanish conqueror of Mexico, to defeat Moctezuma's Aztecs. "Is Licia the reincarnation of La Malinche?" I said.

"Good," Rosa said, like a teacher rewarding a student who had come up with the right answer. "But let's not say 'Malinche.' That name robs her of her singular identity, because, you see, Cortés was also called Malinche by the native people. 'Doña Marina,' her Christian name, also says nothing about who she really was. Let's call her by her true name: Malintzin Tenepal, a Nahuatl princess in the region of the Coatzacoalcos. Sold into slavery by her own widowed mother, who had remarried and wanted only her son to inherit everything. The young Malintzin—almost fifteen when she met Cortés—was given to him as a gift, together with nineteen other young women. She was a gift sent from heaven, and he knew it right away. He used her as his interpreter, in other words, his tongue, ears, and mind. Without her, the Spaniard's mighty sword would have been useless. She was also his lover, friend, comrade-at-arms, and the mother of his son, Martín Cortés."

As she spoke about Malintzin, Rosa's melancholic gaze became more and more animated. Nina had been sitting quietly, listening in earnest. "So, tell us what happened to Malintzin. She must have become a very powerful woman—I mean, she was married to the most powerful man in Mexico," she remarked.

Rosa looked at her. For the first time she smiled fully. "You're right. She did become a powerful woman, but Cortés never married her. Maybe he loved her. Maybe she loved him, too. Who knows? But he wasn't about to marry an Indian woman when he could marry into the Spanish nobility. No. He was an ambitious man. But he gave Malintzin lands and property. Then, when he had no more use for her, he married Malintzin off to one of his captains, Jaramillo."

"How horrible," Nina exclaimed.

"Sooner or later, we all pay for what we do. The law of retribution," Rosa said.

"Where are you from—I mean, originally?" Nina asked abruptly.

From that point, I didn't listen much to the conversation. My stomach was still upset, and I regretted having had so many jalapeños earlier. I also, to say the least, was having a hard time believing that there was any connection between Licia Lecuona and the sixteenth-century Malintzin Tenepal. With the women's superficial similarities—having loveless marriages to men who had squandered their fortunes—the story made for good conversation, but what did it have to do with the attempts on Licia's life?

Rosa seemed quite at ease now, chatting with Nina. Every so often, she threw a glance in my direction. Her change in demeanor and her volunteering so much information about Malintizin's supposed reincarnation into Licia made me suspicious. *She* had asked the question that led us to the subject of Malintzin and Cortés. It occurred to me that she might have been expecting me. If someone had tipped her about my visit, that someone could only be Lester Zamora. Could I have been that wrong about him?

I noticed that Rosa and Nina had stopped talking.

"What is the *fox* thinking now?" Rosa asked me.

"Was Licia . . . Did Licia believe she was the reincarnation of Malintzin when she killed her husband?" I asked bluntly.

Rosa gave me an astonished look.

"Did she believe that?" I pressed.

"Since you answered my question with a question, I'll ask you one: Why are you interested in Licia Román Lecuona?" Her tone was seemingly matter-of-fact, but I could see uneasiness in the way she straightened up in her chair.

"Someone is trying to kill her," I said.

Now, Nina looked at me with surprise. She began to say something, but I signaled for her to keep quiet.

For a few seconds, Rosa Catalino said nothing, then asked, "And how have you come about this information? The newspaper?"

"I was there when it happened."

"Was she badly hurt? Is she okay?"

"*Yes,* to both of your questions," I replied.

"I can't believe anyone would want to kill her now. Do you have any idea who?"

"None. Neither do the police," I answered. "I gather you haven't seen Licia lately."

"Not for the last six months, since I got out of prison."

"Why is that? I understand you and she were very close."

"Yes, we were. But—there was a misunderstanding between us. Nothing serious, but . . ."

"What kind of misunderstanding?"

"Nothing important. Really. I thought she had taken some letters, letters from my daughter and other relatives to me. You see, when you're behind bars, photos and letters become your treasure. I asked her about it, and she said she hadn't. I believed her. But after that incident, she became very distant. We hardly talked."

I noticed that as she talked about the incident in prison, she didn't once look at me or Nina.

"Did you recover them?" I asked.

"What?" she asked, looking briefly at me.

"The letters."

She didn't answer my question right away. Leaning back on her chair, without looking at me, she said, "Yes. A guard—a woman who had a grudge against me—had taken them, just to spite me."

"What made you think Licia had taken your things?"

"Licia and I shared the same cell. I had seen her talking to the guard earlier. I thought . . . maybe . . . It's of no consequence now.

I apologized, but the damage was done," Rosa explained.

"Did this guard have a grudge against Licia, too? Or did an inmate?"

"No. Licia is a very kind, generous person—just as Malintzin Tenepal was." She paused. A minute later, she raised her head. "This attempt on Licia's life is a matter for the police. Why are you involved?"

"I'm not a cop, if that's what you're asking."

"My niece helps people speak well," Nina interjected, unable to keep quiet any longer. "She's a *speech therapist*," she added, helpfully.

I looked at my watch and was surprised to see that we had been there two hours. I pulled out five twenty-dollar bills, walked to the large table in the corner, and left the money there, next to the incense burner.

I turned around as Rosa told Nina, "Tell your niece to look into Malintzin's death. It may give her a clue as to who's trying to kill Licia."

"Oh," Nina exclaimed. "How did she die?"

"Malintzin was found stabbed to death outside her house in Mexico." Rosa looked in my direction. By then, I was sure that she was just trying to impress Nina, perhaps in the hope of gaining another client. Judging by Nina's delight, she had succeeded.

"Time to go, Aunt Nina," I said, gently tugging on her elbow. We began to walk towards the front door.

"Call me, both of you, if you need my assistance again," Rosa said, handing Nina her tape recorder.

Outside, a dog ran after a cat, almost tripping us: The hunter and the hunted. I tried to ignore the cramps radiating from my stomach up to my chest. I looked up and down the street. Someone watched our every move. Helena Zamora? Dora Saldaña?

TWELVE
Purging Previous Sins

I drove Mrs. Contreras home and then rushed to mine. I didn't care if anyone was following me. My body demanded to be made well again. A pulsating pain in my head, behind the bridge of my nose, was making me dizzy. Dropping everything in the hall, I ran into the bathroom. I fell on my knees as I felt a spasm seize my whole body, then another and another until the foul compost in my stomach had emptied itself into the toilet bowl.

I rested my head on the sink cabinet. Perspiring and shivering, I finally got up, undressed, and took a hot shower. Feeling somewhat better, I went upstairs and got in bed. I closed my eyes. Thoughts floated in and out of my mind, but soon I fell into a deep slumber.

A couple of hours later, the phone rang, waking me with a start. My head was still pounding, and the muscles below my ribs ached. But Justin's voice at the other end of the line made me forget my discomfort immediately.

Our conversation was brief. He told me everything was well with him, but he had to be in LA a few more days. I hadn't made much progress, and recounting the day's events wasn't something I was eager to do on an empty, raw stomach and with a pounding head. So I simply said there wasn't much to report.

"Don't give up. Something will turn up, " he said in a reassuring tone. After a few niceties, we said goodnight.

I went down to the kitchen, made some chamomile tea, and warmed up some canned chicken broth. I took an aspirin for my headache. Sipping my tea, I reviewed the few facts I had been able to uncover that day. I ended up going over the same unanswered questions: What role did the Legorretas or the Lecuonas play in the attempt on Licia's life? Had Lester informed Rosa Catalino of my impending visit? Was someone following me? Dora Saldaña? Who was she working for? What about Helena Zamora? So far, she seemed to have the strongest motive for wanting Licia out of the way.

I checked the phone book just in case Helena was listed. A ZAMORA H. listing showed a phone number but no address. When I dialed the number, a perky recorded male voice informed me that I had reached the home of Harvey Zamora. Helena could be living in any of over fifty cities in the San Francisco Bay Area. Well, Justin and I had phone books for every Bay Area county in our office. I quickly got dressed.

As I walked to my car, I looked around in all directions. No other creatures but those within me—the owl and the fox—stirred. I wouldn't have chosen those two animals as symbols of who I was and what I did, but in a way, their skills fit those of my profession.

I started the car and drove slowly for the first two blocks, checking the rearview and side mirrors. A car's headlights turned on two blocks behind me. "Bingo," I said. The driver followed me at a distance, duplicating my turns and speed shifts, until I reached Justin's house on Fruitvale Avenue. The downstairs area was Justin's living quarters. Our office, upstairs, had a separate staircase and entrance.

I ran up the side stairs, went in, and moved quickly to the front window. I didn't see any car pass by and surmised the driver had parked.

I put all the phone books on the desk and turned on the light, and my fingers went to work. My search was unsuccessful. Helena Zamora could have been listed under her maiden name, but I didn't know it. I listened to the messages on the answering machine. Rosenda Mendoza, Lester's secretary, wanted to meet the next day for lunch instead of dinner. I dialed her office number and left a message on her voice mail, confirming a luncheon appointment. Divine Providence was watching over me, for no one knew more about Lester's—and, I hoped, Helena's—life than his personal secretary.

Leaving the desk lamp on, I locked the office and went down the side stairs. Hiding behind the hedge in the front yard, I spotted a black Taurus about half a block down the street. I was considering how to get a closer look when I saw an OPD patrol car cruising slowly down Fruitvale Avenue in our direction. The Taurus, driven by a woman as I had suspected, moved down the street at the maximum speed allowed. I caught only two letters of the license plate: PQ.

My headache was gone, and once home I fell asleep as soon as my head touched the pillow. Towards morning, I found myself re-living my experience at Rosa's house. Inexplicably, the scene shifted. The screech of an owl sent chills up my spine. A horse neighed. Suddenly, again, I felt a sharp pain stab at my left side. I opened my eyes. It was seven-thirty in the morning. I had overslept.

I reached for the phone to call Rafael, Justin's nephew, before he left for school. I wanted him to pay a visit to Melissa, the young receptionist at the Anthropology Department. Perhaps he would succeed where I had failed and convince her to give him Professor Legorreta's home address or phone number.

As I picked up the receiver, I heard the silence of an open line, then noises in the background. "What's going on?" I muttered sleepily.

"Hello. Hello," someone said at the other end. "Is that you, Gloria?"

I recognized Nina's voice. "Hi, Mrs. Contreras," I said. "What's up?"

"I was worried about you. You were so pale and looked sick last night. Are you okay?"

"I'm fine now. I had a touch of the stomach flu or maybe food poisoning."

"Did you throw up?"

"As a matter of fact, I did. Why?"

"I was afraid that would happen," she said. "The first time I went through a past-life regression, I got sick, too. I should have warned you. Nothing wrong with it. It's just a cleansing, a purging of bad karma."

I was tempted to explain that probably *carne asada,* not karma, was the culprit in my case, but I decided against it.

"Anyway. I'm glad you're all right," she said. "I know you're very busy and . . . well, the reason I'm calling is to offer you my help with this case."

Had I created a monster, I wondered.

Sensing my hesitation, she said, "Before you say no, let me tell you what I had in mind. Remember that Sister Rosa suggested you look into Malintzin's death for clues as to who's trying to kill Black . . . Licia? Well, I . . . No, *Pita* and I thought we can go to the library and find that information for you. What do you think?"

I smiled at the thought of the two *comadres,* my mother and Mrs. Contreras, in pursuit of the legendary Malinche. Although I felt that Rosa's suggestion was only a ploy to steer me away from her, there was no risk involved here. Nina's offer was difficult to resist. I only hoped they would not try to take their investigation outside the library.

Nina was delighted when I agreed. "We'll be calling you later with our first progress report," she chirped.

By the time I called Rafael's house, he had already left for class. I got dressed and drove to his high school, Oakland Tech.

I remembered fondly when my father, a Tech alumnus and lifetime Bulldogs fan, had taken me on a tour of the school. He had tried, unsuccessfully, to convince me to attend there instead of Fremont High, by running down a list of Tech's illustrious alumni: Congressman Ron Dellums, Clint Eastwood, The Pointer Sisters, symphony conductor Antonia Brico, and poet Rod McKuen, among others.

As I drove down Broadway, past the huge main building, I admired its stately Greek-inspired architecture, now painted a dull yellow.

I parked on Fortieth Street and made my way to the east gate. Like most public school campuses, Oakland Tech had an open-door policy: All its gates and entrances were kept unlocked during school hours. An invitation to strangers, I thought, as a tall Latino-looking man, walkie-talkie in hand and dressed in suit and tie, approached when he caught sight of me. As he approached, however, he kept his eyes on a group of young men standing by the girls' gym. All were wearing plaid shirts and baggy pants of the same color. Homeboys.

When they saw the man in the suit, all except one began to walk out the gate with a slow, uniform stride. They got into a car parked across the street, next to mine. One slid behind the wheel, started the car, and waited. The young man who had stayed now crossed his arms, and I noticed a bulky object under his shirt. He was carrying a weapon. I felt my arms and legs tense up. The man in the suit still moved towards the younger one. He lowered his arms but kept both his hands on his belt. The homeboy spit on the ground and turned around when he saw a black-and-white pull up next to the suited man. Still taking his time, he walked towards the waiting car. The two men talked briefly while the homeboys' car darted out with a screech.

"Who were those guys? Do they go to school here?" I asked the man in the suit as I caught up to him.

"No. They're not students. They're members of the Border Brothers. They and the Crips are two of our gangs. They come to recruit," he answered, wiping his forehead with his handkerchief. "What can I do for you?" he asked, walking up the steps towards the main building.

"I'm looking for Rafael Escobar. He's a student here."

He looked at his watch. "It's almost time for the bell. Come with me to the main office and get a pass. The secretary will tell you where to find Rafael," he suggested. As we walked, a few students, milling around in the halls, scurried back into classrooms or took off in the opposite direction when they saw him.

There was something vaguely familiar about him and I looked at his ID card. He was the dean of students and his name was Pablo C. Ramírez. I'd had a teacher by that name at Fremont High back in 1968. My friend Luisa and I had led a student walk-out when the Board of Education had threatened to fire him and two black teachers for teaching us Mexican and African-American history. I asked him if by chance he was that teacher.

He looked at me inquisitively. A glimmer of recognition showed in his eyes. "Gloria, right?"

"One and the same."

"Of course."

I nodded and smiled.

"A small world," he said, but the bell rang at that moment, and Mr. Ramírez's attention shifted to the throngs of students filling the halls to capacity. He suddenly turned his attention to a couple of male students who had unlit cigarettes hanging from their lips. "Put those away. You have five minutes to get to your next class. Hubba hubba."

"God's spoken," one of the students said and laughed. Although they didn't rush to their next class, they nonetheless put the cigarettes back in the pack.

As the secretary was checking the computer to locate Rafael's next class, a call came through Mr. Ramirez's walkie-talkie. He listened, then said, "On my way." Turning to the secretary, he said, "Please, call 911. We need the paramedics."

He waved at me and rushed away down the hall. He should be wearing a police uniform, not a suit, I thought.

Ten minutes later, I found Rafael on the athletic field. He was the only Chicano member of the Bulldogs—a rarity since Chicanos and Latinos were not often recruited to play football. He was also an honor student and most importantly my hope to get Professor Legorreta's address.

I briefly explained what the situation was and gave him the slip of paper with Melissa's phone number and office hours.

"I'll get to it right after school," he said.

As I walked back across the campus to my car, I saw the paramedics, an OPD officer, and Mr. Ramírez on their knees, bending over a young man who was lying on the cold ground.

Standing a short distance away was a young woman, tears running down her cheeks. "I told him not to do it," she told her girl friends, who were trying to comfort her. "I told him not to smoke that. I saw Jabbal and his friends soaking their joints in embalming fluid yesterday. But he wouldn't listen. And now Otis dead. I know he's dead. And where is Jabbal? He not even a student here. They never catch him."

What previous sins were all we paying for, I wondered. Something was terribly wrong when our future lay lifeless on cold November ground, drowned in a fluid meant only to preserve the dead.

THIRTEEN
Decanted Souls

Walking into La Ultima restaurant, I looked forward to rekindling my friendship with Rosenda Mendoza. But I also dreaded having to talk about our friend Luisa's death. Two years before, Luisa had stepped between me and a bullet, giving up her life for mine. I realized that my remorse and grief at her death were also part of the sediment weighing heavily on my soul during and after the attempt on Licia Lecuona's life. Witnessing today's events at Oakland Tech had made matters worse. At the restaurant, waiting for Rosenda, even the *sangría* I had ordered seemed dispirited.

My friend walked into the restaurant ten minutes later. We spent a good hour reminiscing about our childhood in Jingletown. As I'd expected, we talked about Luisa and the way she died.

Rosenda patted my hand and said, "But isn't it wonderful she left us her poetry, her very soul—to always remember her by?"

Words tied themselves up in my throat, and I fell silent. I was glad when she changed the subject and began talking about her life as a single working mother. Doing clerical work to support her oldest daughter and herself, she had managed to graduate from college. Brimming with happiness and love, she also told me how she and her husband had met and married, and had finally relocated to the Bay Area.

"How did you end up working for Lester Zamora?" I asked.

"Some years ago, my husband was accused of embezzling. Someone recommended Lester to us. We liked him and hired him. At the time, Lester's secretary had just quit, so he asked us to write a narrative of the case for him. I did that and also gathered all sorts of documents for him to support my husband's innocence. Lester won the case for us. He was impressed with my work and offered me a job. I was between jobs and I accepted. He's a wonderful person. Compassionate, witty, doesn't take himself seriously, which is nice. But make no mistake, he is an excellent litigator."

"He strikes me as a caring father but a very lonely man."

"I suppose so. Plenty of women are interested in him, and he goes out on dates every so often. He just hasn't found the right woman."

"Maybe he's still in love with his former wife. I understand they're divorced."

"I'm not sure he's still in love with her. He does care a lot about her and feels obligated. He certainly sends her a considerable amount in alimony every month. I know. I send the checks. After all, she's Xochitl's mother . . ."

Although the restaurant was now almost empty, Rosenda lowered her voice. She told me that Helena Zamora had been a very jealous wife and verbally abusive to Lester in public. Her displays of jealousy hadn't done much good for his career. She had even tried to get him disbarred, claiming that he'd had a long affair with one of his clients. *Licia,* I thought. Rosenda reassured me that Lester had always been good to Helena and had never raised a hand to hurt her.

"He might have told you that I was at his home last night," I said. "Why aren't there any photos of Helena in the Zamora house?"

"She tore every photo of herself into little pieces," Rosenda said in a whisper. About six months before, after an appointment with her doctor, Helena Zamora had packed up her essentials and had left Lester and Xochitl. The next thing he heard, she was in a hospital.

"Her doctor told her she had ALS. I guess that's all she could take and she tried to commit suicide," Rosenda said.

"What's that?" I asked.

"Amyotrophic Lateral Sclerosis—Lou Gehrig's disease."

I realized that Helena could not be the person attempting to kill Licia. Anyone afflicted with ALS would have an incredibly hard time moving around, let alone having the strength to plunge a knife into someone else's shoulder. She could have hired someone to do it for her, but the idea seemed far-fetched.

"Where is Helena Zamora now?" I asked.

"She lives with her parents in Denver," Rosenda replied. She began to ask me all sorts of questions about my decision to become a private investigator. When her curiosity was satisfied, she asked, "Have you ever done any work for attorneys? I mean— I was thinking that maybe you could work for us, too. Our firm uses the services of private investigators every so often."

"Justin, my partner, and I have done work for various attorneys from time to time, mostly for divorce lawyers, that sort of thing. But I'm sure we could handle other kinds of cases," I answered. "Does your firm do business with Ace Security and Investigations in San Leandro?" I asked, trying to sound as casual as possible.

"As a matter of fact, we do. Why do you ask?"

"Nothing important, really," I said. "But I've heard that a Chicana works for them. It's nice to know I'm not the only one in this business."

"That's great. I guess we've come a long way after all," Rosenda remarked. "Who is she?"

"I believe her name is Dora Saldaña."

"Hmm . . . come to think of it, there is a woman who calls Lester on his private line. Her call came through reception once, and Mrs. Cartier told me that this woman was a private investigator. I can't recall her name now. But at Ace, we've mostly dealt with the head honcho."

About three-thirty, Rosenda and I parted, promising not to lose touch with each other again and to take flowers to Luisa's grave.

When I got home, I called my mother. She and Nina Contreras had enjoyed a busy day at the library, she informed me, and asked me to drop by her house so they could "brief" me on their "findings."

Two hours later, Rafael called. He had finally gotten a phone number and address for the Legorretas, who lived in Livermore, a city southeast of Oakland, better known for the nuclear lab operated there by the University of California. Pretending to be selling subscriptions to the local paper, Rafael had called the number Melissa had given him, confirming that they were still in town. He had also gotten directions from Melissa to get there. The young woman had been to the Legorreta's house, together with other students, as the professor was fond of inviting students to his house to view his collection of pre-Columbian artifacts.

"To get to their house, you're going to have to go around the Lienzo Charro. It's that place where the *charros* have their annual rodeo," he said.

"Yes. I remember. My father used to take us there horseback-riding and to the rodeos," I said, then congratulated Rafael on his thoroughness.

"Gloria, we're having two half-days at school, tomorrow and Friday. The teachers have in-service training. If there's anything else you want me to do, let me know. Anyway, could you pay me for these hours today? I promised Melissa I would take her out to dinner."

"Business or pleasure?"

"Pleasure, of course," he said with a chuckle. "We really hit it off."

"Then dinner is on me," I told him. "Give me about an hour. I'll leave a check for you in Justin's mailbox. But there *is* someone I'd like you to keep an eye on—that is, when I find her."

"Okay. Later then," Rafael said.

I freshened up my make-up and brushed my hair, then carefully gathered it with a band and bow into a low pony tail. Wanting to appear trustworthy and professional, I put on a light cowl neck sweater and a two-piece wool flannel pantsuit. Matching pumps and handbag completed the outfit. To round up my look, I pulled my briefcase out of the coat closet.

After a brief stop at the office to drop off Rafael's check, I drove to my mother's house on Thirty-fifth Avenue in the

Fruitvale District. I rang the bell to announce my presence, then unlocked the door with my key to her house. My mother insisted that I always carry that key with me in case of emergency.

"You look so attractive, Gloria," Nina said. Removing some books from an easy chair, she added, "Sit here. Read these pages." She handed me two old volumes in which she had bookmarked some passages with, respectively, a comb, a nail file, a pencil, and a variety of hairpins.

"I'm taking these books and your notes with me. I can't read all this in one sitting," I complained. "I have to go to Livermore in a little while."

"Pita, do you think maybe we can just give her a *report*?" Nina asked my mother. "We have plenty of notes."

"That's a very good idea, Nina," my mother replied. "Let's go into the kitchen. We can have something to eat while we do that."

"You understand that we've just *begun*," my mother warned as she put a bowl of steamy *cocido* in front of me. I looked at the rich beef and vegetable soup topped with fresh avocado and knew that it was just what my spirit and stomach needed. "Still, it's amazing how little the history books say about Malintzin. We've looked in the indexes of many books at the library. The librarians suggested that. We brought home only those books that mentioned her name. But Malinche is hardly *mentioned* in history books."

"It's unfair," Nina commented. "I mean . . . after all, without Malinche's intervention, Hernán Cortés would have been killed by the Cholulans. He wouldn't have been able to talk with the Aztecs or anyone else in Mexico. But most of what Sister Rosa said is true. Malintzin was sold into slavery by her own mother. Can you *imagine*? Her own *mother.* When she was only fifteen, she and other girls were given to Hernán Cortés. At first Cortés didn't want her and gave her to his favorite captain, Puertocarreño. But he soon found out that Malintzin was not only good-looking and good-natured, she was smart and knew many Indian languages. She also learned Spanish very fast. Cortés sent Puertocarreño on an errand to Spain and took Malintzin as his mistress . . ."

"I'm glad you're saying she was his mistress not his *girlfriend,* like you told me earlier," my mother interjected. "Really, Nina."

Ignoring my mother's remark, Nina went on to add a multitude of details about Cortés's alliance with many tribes that hated the Aztecs, which had enabled the Spaniards to triumph over them.

"And who was there, by his side, wiping his tears after his first defeat by the Aztecs, the battle of La Noche Triste?" Mrs. Contreras asked. "Malintzin, of course."

My mother voiced her protest about the way Mexican historians had reviled La Malinche, presenting her as a traitor to her people. "How about all those Tlaxcalteca warriors who fought the Aztecs alongside Cortes's army?" she asked. "No-o-o-o. They were men. Men do not betray. Ha!"

As she spoke, my mother's face flushed as if she were seized by a sudden fever. Without noticing it, she had switched to English, a habit of hers when something made her truly angry.

"Except for Bernal Díaz. He always writes about 'Doña Marina' with such respect and admiration," she added, referring to one of Cortés's soldiers who had written a chronicle of the conquest of Mexico.

"I think Bernal Díaz was in love with Malintzin," Nina said.

"You do, eh? I do, too," my mother agreed. They smiled at each other.

I could see where their conversation was going. "I hate to interrupt, but you were supposed to find out how Malinche died. Any information about that?"

"You expect miracles," my mother protested. "I told you we've only just begun. Go on to your appointment. We'll give you a second report tomorrow."

"Okay. Call me if you come across any new information," I said as we all walked to the front door.

Kissing them both on the cheek, I told them how much I appreciated their efforts. Their glowing faces accompanied me on my journey up the dark Livermore hills in search of Legorreta's house.

FOURTEEN
Furies in the Mist

It was a moonless, misty November evening. The winding road I had been following up the hill was fenced in on each side. Every so often, I saw gates barring visitors from the houses hidden in the mist. The smell of horse manure coming through the car vents worked its way up my nostrils. Lowering the window, I heard whinnying in the distance, and I knew I was on the right track. But I was also reminded of the events on the Day of the Dead. Who were the horsemen? Who was the woman in black?

I came to the entrance to a long driveway and stopped. The house, about fifty feet away, sat on the brow of a hill. I immediately noticed the realtor's sign. The house was being sold. I got out of the car briefly and double-checked the name on the mailbox. Why were the Legorretas moving? Where?

I heard the noise of a car coming up the road behind me. I listened intently. The car stopped, but I could still hear its engine. It couldn't be very far back, but the mist made it impossible to see clearly. Suddenly, the car started up the hill again.

I drove into the Legorretas' driveway until I found a spot off the road where I could hide from view. I parked and turned off the engine, waiting for the other car to go past, but it didn't. I got out of the car. Moving slowly through some of the brush along the driveway, I soon spotted the other car coming up towards the house. It was the Taurus.

The driver stopped at almost the same spot I had before. Someone got out and looked around. When the interior light of the car stayed off, I realized that the driver was taking precautions. Although I couldn't see her clearly, I had a strong feeling that I was laying eyes on Dora Saldaña for the first time. I began to move closer, but just when I was a few feet away, she got back into her car, turned, and headed in the opposite direction.

I went back to my car. I opened and secured the hood. Turning on my flashlight, I loosened one of the connecting cables to the distributor to disable my car. I closed the hood gently and put the flashlight back in the car.

As I approached the front door, I noticed a red VW Jetta and a blue Volvo station wagon parked behind each other along the driveway. I straightened my pants, buttoned my coat, and rang the bell. A handsome young man, no older than nineteen, opened the door. After looking me over, he took a step out and checked the area on both sides of the door.

Changing my briefcase from one hand to another so he would notice it, I said, "I'm sorry to bother you, but I wonder if I may use your phone. I got lost trying to find a client's house down the road, and my car stalled. I have to call my road service."

The door was opened wider by an older woman, who I assumed was Mrs. Legorreta—Peter Lecuona's sister and Licia's sister-in-law.

"What is it?" she asked. She was joined at the door by a young woman, perhaps only a year younger than her brother. The children looked a great deal like each other, but bore little resemblance to their mother. The young man told his mother briefly what I'd said.

"Please, come in," she said, pulling the door completely open. "You can use the phone in the study. This way." Her voice was low-pitched, with no trace of any accent.

A tall attractive woman, in her mid-fifties and a bit overweight, Mrs. Legoreta had a soft manner but hunched a little as she walked. What struck me most about her was her sad countenance. I wondered if life with Juan Gabriel Legorreta had been unhappy.

Along the hallway, I noticed the many boxes, crates, and wrapping supplies.

Isabela Legorreta showed me to the study. It was a large room with bookcases lining the walls and long showcases taking most of the space between them. There was a large desk near a window, opposite the door. Nothing was disturbed in this room.

Mrs. Legorreta didn't come in, but simply pointed at the phone on the desk. I walked slowly, stopping briefly to admire the pre-Columbian artifacts and jewels in the softly illuminated glass cases. I looked in my wallet for my road-service card and dialed the number on it.

Knowing that she was just outside the door, I asked her for her address. She came in, followed by her children. I handed her the receiver and asked her if she wouldn't mind giving directions to her house to the road-service operator. She did as I requested, then handed me back the phone.

"They'll be here in a half-hour," I said as I put my card back in my wallet. "I hate to impose, but my client is probably wondering what happened to me. Would you mind if I called her?"

Mrs. Legorreta nodded and signaled for the children to follow her out of the room. I dialed my number at home and pretended to have a conversation with my fictitious client.

When I stepped out of the study, Mrs. Legorreta's children were waiting outside the door. "My mother wants to know if you'd like some coffee or something to drink," the young woman said. Although I felt like a spy in the house of kindness, I accepted.

"Martín, tell Mom she wants coffee," she told her brother, then ushered me to the living room. Half-packed crates stood in disarray around the room. I sat on the sofa while the young woman relaxed in an armchair, with one of her legs draped over the arm.

"My name is Gloria," I said.

"I'm Inés," she replied. "Nice to meet you."

"How interesting. My middle name is Inés, too," I commented. "But I hear that name only when my mother gets mad at me."

Inés smiled. She seemed almost as old as her brother, but she smiled more than him. "How old are you?" I asked.

"Almost eighteen," she answered. "Martín is almost eighteen, too," she volunteered.

"No wonder you look so much alike," I said.

Inés gave me a puzzled look, then giggled.

From then on, the questions and answers centered around her plans for college. She and Martín were applying for admission at Stanford and they were hoping to rent an apartment together, now that her parents were moving to Mexico. But their parents were not in favor of that move. They wanted them to go to college in Mexico.

Mrs. Legorreta walked into the room with a tray. Martín was right behind her.

"We're going to watch MTV for a while," Inés said, getting up. "C'mon, Martín, let's go," she told her brother, nudging him.

"Chill," Martín said, but smiled and followed her to the door.

Mrs. Legorreta looked at them with concern.

"I know. We'll turn it off when Father gets home," Inés said.

"Your children are beautiful," I said. I looked at my watch.

"You still have time to finish your coffee," Mrs. Legorreta said, as she poured some coffee into two cups and handed one to me.

"You have a beautiful collection of jewels and artifacts," I said.

"Thank you. My husband is the collector. He's a professor of anthropology at Cal. By the way, my name is Isabela Legorreta," she said and stretched her hand out to me. I shook it as I gave her my maiden name.

"He must have been collecting for a long time. Some of those jewelry pieces are outstanding," I remarked.

"Yes. It's been his lifelong passion. What do you do?"

"I'm an attorney. I've had my own practice, but it's been very hard to make it on my own. I'll be joining a firm in Oakland soon," I said.

"Oh, how nice. We have some friends who are lawyers in Oakland as well. What's the name of the firm you'll be joining?"

"Scott, Cartier and Foreman," I said as casually as I could manage. "A friend of mine, Lester Zamora, who's also an attorney with them, was able to convince them to take a chance and hire me. Do you know any of them?"

Isabela Legorreta was about to take a sip of her coffee when I mentioned Lester's name. Her hand began to shake visibly, making the cup and saucer rattle. She put them on the table. Raising her hand, she pressed her fingers against her cheek as if her teeth ached.

"Are you feeling all right?" I asked. "Did I say something wrong?"

"No. I'm all right. It's just . . . We . . . my family . . . He was the attorney who defended the woman who murdered my brother."

"I'm terribly sorry. I didn't know," I said, feeling two inches tall, for she seemed so vulnerable. "I hope you don't mind my asking, but who was the woman who killed your brother?"

"Her name is Licia Román. She was my brother Peter's wife," she answered. "I'm sorry. I shouldn't be telling you this," she said, taking a deep breath.

"Nothing to be sorry about," I offered. "Did the woman go free?"

"No. She went to jail for a long time." Slumping a little, she looked in my direction, but her gaze slid past me to some spot behind me. "She paid for her crime."

"It didn't happen recently then," I said.

"No. But it feels like it happened yesterday. You see, she's *out* now."

"Are you afraid that she might come after you? Is that why you're moving?"

Isabela sighed, then, finally focusing on me, answered, "No. No. It's just . . . It's all been like a bad dream. A nightmare . . . Peter and I were very close, as close as children can be to each other."

She straightened up, and I put down my cup and saucer on the table. An instant later, we both heard the loud noise of a car engine. When I didn't hear the sound of a horn, I assumed it wasn't the road-service truck. I cursed under my breath.

Inés rushed into the room, followed by Martín. They both sat down on the sofa, next to their mother. The easy-going, relaxed attitude they'd both shown before suddenly changed to anxious stares and stiff poses. Inés looked at me briefly—but long enough for me to read terror in her eyes.

We heard the car go into the garage, next to the living room. The house shuddered lightly as a door slammed, telling everyone the professor was in the house. Martín's eyes narrowed and his voice deepened, as he said, "Father's here."

"Did you turn the TV off?" Isabela asked in a tense but low voice.

Inés whispered, "Yes."

A minute later, a dark-complected man of medium build and dressed in a suit and tie came into the room. The two women stood up. But Martín remained seated. I gathered my handbag and briefcase and also rose slowly to my feet.

"What have we here?" he said, looking me over. "A social worker?"

Without waiting for a response, he looked at the children. "Go and finish your packing."

Inés was the first one to leave the room with hurried steps. She looked briefly at her father as she went past him. But Martín walked out with a purposely slow stride and indolent attitude, looking straight ahead.

I instinctively moved closer to Isabela Legorreta until my arm was barely touching hers. She took a deep breath and, with a slightly quavering voice, said, "This is Miss Vélez, dear. She's an attorney. Her car—"

Juan Gabriel Legorreta interrupted her. "A lawyer. 'Kill all the lawyers.'" He looked directly at me. The corner of his upper lip rose slightly. "Shakespeare," he added.

I held his gaze. "Nice to meet you." Isabela went on to explain my reason for being there, but made no mention of our conversation about Lester Zamora. Instead, she said, "Miss Vélez was just telling me how much she admires your collection."

"Do you know anything about pre-Columbian art, Miss Vélez?" he asked with a slightly softer voice.

"Not much," I answered. "In college, I took a course in cultural anthropology. We briefly studied some pre-Columbian cultures. Unfortunately—"

"Cultural anthropology . . . You mean *folklore*," he interjected. "Hardly anthropology, is it?"

I was putting together a polite response when he added, "You Mexicans—Chicanos—you are so ignorant. You don't value what you have."

"I suppose that's why you feel that any Juan has the right to walk away with Mexico's national treasure," I snapped back.

He glared not at me but at his wife. Isabela tensed up and stretched her hand towards her husband, but he pushed it away. I briefly looked at a long scar on the back of his hand and relished the notion that perhaps Isabela or one of the children had put it there. We seemed to have become a frozen tableau when the honking of a horn sounded. The road-service truck had arrived.

Before I started for the door, I turned to Isabela. Following an impulse, I put one arm around her and gave her a loose hug. "Thank you," I said. Close to her ear, I whispered, "You're a very good person." She attempted a smile.

"Such familiarity," Professor Legorreta said. As the door closed behind me, I heard him add, "I've warned you about letting in strangers." A slap, then silence, followed the warning.

Regret and rage mixed in my stomach. My visit to the Legorreta household had yielded little. I still had no clue as to why Juan Gabriel Legorreta might want Licia dead. I would have loved to charge back into the house, and, like a Don Quixote, do battle with Legorreta. But I regretfully had grown beyond Quixote's eminent foolhardiness.

FIFTEEN
Abstract of Death

Fueled by a powerful dose of anger, and oblivious to my own safety, I drove downhill quite fast. I sobered up when, coming to a sharp bend, I almost lost control. I took a second sharp twist on the road at a safer speed and saw the headlights of another car behind me, closing in.

"Not this time," I said under my breath. I slowed down yet again, waiting for the other car to get closer. By the shape and dark color, I sensed it was the Taurus. I took a flashlight out of my glove compartment and sandwiched it between my handbag and the back of the passenger seat. Then, I stepped on the gas. The other car shadowed my moves. For a while, we were like downhill racers speeding towards Hell.

We were almost at the bottom of the hill, where the road began to widen. I knew I was near the intersection, so I sped up. As expected, the other driver did, too. Without stepping on the brake, I shifted to a lower gear. The engine heaved under the pressure, coming almost to a halt. I slammed on the brakes and braced for an impact.

Faced with a collision, the driver of the other car swerved to avoid me. In vain. I heard the screeching of the brakes, the thundering of metal, against metal, the sound of glass shattering. I held onto the wheel. Pain zigzagged up my arm to the back of my neck, as I saw the black Taurus brush against the side of the hill and make a complete spin around.

I quickly unbuckled my seatbelt, reached for the flashlight, and got out of the car. I could hear the Taurus's engine still humming.

I expected the driver to get out of the car. She didn't. I began to run towards it. I was as concerned for her safety as I was afraid of a violent confrontation. But I didn't have time to find out which troubled me more. She backed her car up, turned, and headed down the road. But not soon enough. Flashing my light on her license plate, I was able to see the letters and numbers on it, except for the last digit.

"Gotcha," I said, as I reached in my handbag for my memo pad and pen. I wrote down the license plate number, then reached in my bag again for a handkerchief to wipe the sweat off my forehead and neck. I leaned back on my car, trying to catch my breath. A bit calmer, I inspected the damage to the left rear fender, which wasn't as bad as I'd feared. The taillight cover was intact. In general, my car was running well, so I drove slowly down to the intersection and parked off the road.

I immediately phoned my insurance agent. Justin and I had done some free work for her the year before, and she owed us a favor.

After telling her what happened, I gave her the license number and asked her to get the driver's name and address for me.

"Listen, Gloria. You'll still have to file a police report early tomorrow morning, if you don't want to do it now, or I won't be able to get your car repaired soon," she warned.

"I will. Tomorrow. First thing. But I really need that name and address," I said. "It's urgent."

As I pushed the cell phone's power-button off with my thumb, pain rushed again up my arm to the back of my neck. I became aware of every muscle in my arms and legs aching. But what stunned me was not pain but a sudden, overwhelming conviction that, no matter how many people loved me, I would be alone at the hour of my death. No abstract belief in future lives or heaven could fill the emptiness I felt in the wake of that sensation.

Half an hour later, I walked into my house. After downing a shot of tequila straight up—something I hardly ever did—I checked my voice-mail messages.

"He killed her," I heard my mother say. "He choked her to

death. But he said that she died in her sleep, even though the marks of her pearl necklace were all around her neck." My heart jumped. For an instant, I believed my mother was somehow talking about Licia Lecuona. I relaxed only when she went on to say, "But Cortés was already so powerful in Mexico that, even if people didn't believe that Catalina, his first wife, died of natural causes, they couldn't do anything about it. Imagine. All the time that Catalina lived in Coyoacán with him, Malinche was living there, too. So far, *nothing* about Malinche's death. We'll call you tomorrow."

I could hear the irritation in my mother's voice, but also her excitement. Even if she and Nina Contreras didn't uncover anything that could help me, I felt they were thrilled with their incursion into Mexican history. I hated to admit that Legorreta—echoing Rosa Catalino—had been right when he said that we Chicanos were proud of our ancestors, but had little idea what our heritage was all about. It was unsettling that two people so different and yet so proud of Mexico's heritage were precisely the ones who felt the most contempt for us.

A second phone message from Justin simply said hello. I missed him more than ever.

SIXTEEN
Only a Native Girl

The next morning, I phoned Rafael and asked him to check with me at the end of his school day. If my insurance agent was able to get me the name and address of the woman following me, I would ask him to keep an eye on her. When I finally talked to my insurance agent, she seemed somewhat reluctant to give me the information.

"Look, if my client weren't in danger, I wouldn't be asking you to do this for me."

"All right! The owner of your mystery car is Dora Saldaña. She lives at 5687 Moraga Court. I think that's in the Montclair Area. But, Gloria, unless you get a police report, we can't proceed."

"Relax. First, I want to go by her house and make sure that hers is the car in question. Then, I'll go to the police." What I didn't tell her was that I intended to use my insurance claim as leverage to get the information I wanted.

After I showered, I called Michael Cisneros's office. His secretary was expecting my call and gave me an appointment for three o'clock that afternoon. Then, I decided to pay a visit to Dora Saldaña.

Dora lived in a small cottage behind a larger house on Moraga Court, a short U-shaped street that began and ended on Mountain Boulevard, close to the bustling Montclair shopping district. A small rose garden separated the main house from the cottage. The main house had one garage, and I assumed that Dora had to park on the street, but the black Taurus was nowhere to be seen.

Since my encounter the night before, I had been feeling anxious and distraught. In fact, something unusual had been at work in me ever since the Day of the Dead, when I had laid eyes on Black Widow for the first time. Most powerful was the sense that my death might be imminent. From previous experience, I knew that the only cure for such feelings was to keep moving. Since I couldn't do that at the moment, I looked around for something to read. The history books my mother and Nina had given me were still in the trunk. I took them out and began to read the passages about Malinche that they had marked for me.

One book was a translation of Hernán Cortés's letters to the King of Spain during the conquest of Mexico. Cortés related his efforts on behalf of the crown to obtain treasure and described his efforts, strategy, and the struggle that finally led his few hundred Spanish soldiers to defeat the Aztecs. He made mention of Malinche only twice throughout his many letters, referring to her as a young native woman who served, together with Aguilar, as his interpreter. This woman had been not only his interpreter and lover, she had also saved him and his men from getting killed by the Cholulans. Yet Cortés was not only married already but also a professed Catholic. He had to play down Malinche's role so no one would question his integrity.

I began to wonder what Malinche thought and felt. Had she also used Cortés to gain power? Had she loved him or simply been fascinated by him and his world? Was she moved by her contempt for the Aztecs, who had extracted tribute and sacrifices from the other peoples in Mexico? When she converted to Catholicism, had she done so because she wanted so much to believe in a God kinder than the bloody Huitzilopochtli, who demanded human sacrifice?

Regardless of her motives, one thing seemed certain: Malinche—even as young as she was when she met Cortés—had been a complex woman. She was surely the most maligned and misunderstood woman in the history of Mexico: To say *malinchista* to someone in modern Mexico was equivalent to calling someone a Benedict Arnold in the United States.

As I perused the other books, I also realized that Malinche

had disappeared from the record when she was no longer of any use to Cortés. After he left Mexico, she lived the rest of her life in obscurity. I wondered who had killed Malinche—if indeed she'd been stabbed to death, as Rosa Catalino suggested. How had she died? What, if anything, did her death have to do with Black Widow? The only one who could answer those questions was Licia herself.

It was nearly two in the afternoon when I decided that Dora Saldaña wasn't coming home just yet. I called Rafael, arranged for him to continue the surveillance, and on his arrival I headed home before my appointment with Michael Cisneros at three.

As I walked into my house, I heard Nina's voice speaking into the answering machine. "Cortés took their son Martín away from Malinche. He is getting ready to go back to Spain, so what does he do? He marries Malinche off to a *drunken captain* named Jaramillo. I suppose, as a mother, she wanted Martín to have everything he was entitled to as Hernán Cortés's son." After another brief pause, she added, "You know, Octavio Paz is a great writer, but even he calls Malintzin *la gran chingada*. I didn't know that the word *chingada* means the Indian woman raped by the conqueror. No wonder we Mexicans consider it the worst of all insults."

Driving to Michael Cisneros's office in Jingletown, I realized it was almost a week since the attempt on Licia's life and I wasn't any closer to discovering the identity of her would-be killer. I couldn't find any motive for either Rosa Catalino or Lester Zamora to want Licia dead. Licia had withdrawn her friendship from Rosa, but her action hardly constituted a reason for revenge; while Lester had remained Licia's staunchest supporter and friend for all those years. Losing her case had obviously not impeded his career. Helena Zamora, afflicted with Lou Gehrig's disease, was now off my list altogether. Isabela Legorreta struck me as a woman who would rather suffer than make others suffer. Nonetheless, she had been extremely troubled by even the mention of Lester's name. And Juan Gabriel Legorreta was certainly capable of cruelty. But why would he go after Licia? He might be after Licia's money, but that would mean filing a wrongful-death suit. Why try to kill Licia? It didn't make any sense.

Half an hour later, Michael's secretary showed me into his office. As always, he greeted me with a smile and a hearty handshake. After giving him my rather skimpy report, I said, "Other than talking directly with Licia, my only hope is to meet with Dora Saldaña and find out who hired her and why. Have your people been able to find out anything about her?"

"My people tell me she was always very professional. Most of the time, however, the reports came from the head of ASI," he replied. "We have no idea what business Licia could possibly have had with her."

"Licia might not want to see me, but I've been wondering if you could arrange a meeting between us. She might know something, perhaps remember something about her assailant, that might help me locate this person."

Michael was lost in thought for a while. "I talked to her this morning. She is determined to leave the Bay Area and travel for some time. I convinced her to delay her trip for a few days. But since I couldn't convince her not to do it at all, I did talk her into accepting a Travelling companion. I'm thinking that . . ."

"I might be that companion," I interjected.

Michael smiled, reached out, and tapped my hand. "Yes. You might be just what she needs now. I know you're probably quite busy, but since you're already involved to some degree . . ."

"It makes sense."

"Very good," Michael said, pleased. "I'll be responsible for all of your travel expenses. If you need another check, let my secretary know."

As soon as I got back in my car, I called Justin in Los Angeles.

"It all sounds intriguing. But it also seems like a very risky enterprise," he said. "This woman has already killed a man and seems quite delusional. If she still has to report to a probation officer, you could be charged with aiding a fugitive. Drugs might be involved. In addition, you might have to deal with whomever is trying to kill her. But you've already made up your mind, haven't you?"

"I want to do it."

"Not much to discuss then," Justin told me. "Take the .38. And be careful."

"I love you," I said, following an impulse. It was the first time I had said those words to him.

"I'm a lucky man," he said.

I packed an overnight bag with clothes, toiletries, a flashlight, my compass—a gift from my father I always took with me on trips—my cellular phone, and the gun Justin had suggested. I also made sure I had the mace cannister I always carried in my hand-bag.

I had at last made my feelings clear to Justin. Had I done so only because I was going to my grave now? I wondered, as I drove up the hill towards Black Widow's house.

SEVENTEEN
The Wingless Firefly

Banging on the iron gate and pressing the buzzer got me nowhere. The lights were off and the drapes drawn. There were no signs of life inside or outside Licia's Victorian house.

Had I misunderstood Michael Cisneros? Or had Licia agreed to his suggestions just to keep him off her back? Had she already fled? I fumbled with the padlock at the entrance. To my surprise, it was unlocked. I slid it off the ring, then pushed the gate open. I went back to my car. From the overnight bag, I took out my gun and flashlight, and from my wallet my P.I. identification and driver's license. I slid the gun between my belt and the waist of my pants.

Holding the mace in my left hand and the flashlight in the right, I walked through the gate. I put back the padlock as I had found it. I looked around the grounds, then walked up the steps to the front door. The door was ajar, and I pushed it until it gently bounced against the wall. Trying to control my breathing and the shaking of my hands, I waited. I stood in place and let my eyes and ears get used to the darkness. I heard only the comforting hum of kitchen appliances. For an old house, the Victorian was hardly noisy. A nightlight at the bottom of a staircase flickered as if sensing my approach.

When I felt somewhat safe, I turned the flashlight on and began to inspect my surroundings. I was in the living area of the house. Next to it was the dining room. A door beyond it probably connected with the kitchen. Between the living and dining areas I saw the flight of stairs leading most likely to the bedrooms. Looking up the stairwell, I said, softly at first, then louder, "Hello. Anyone home?" I waited. No one answered.

I was getting ready to go back to the car and phone Michael, when I heard creaking sounds above me: It was the noise of someone's cautious footsteps. I waited. I turned off the flashlight and put it away. Holding the mace cannister in my hand, I began to climb up the steps, my back against the wall so I could have an unobstructed view. My heart was pounding hard. Adrenalin welled up in my temples, and the pressure around my eyes mounted, making them pulsate.

Reaching a landing, I stopped to catch my wits and breath. I decided to put the mace cannister in my pants pocket and took out the gun instead. I resumed my climb. At the top of the stairs, lit by a small wall lamp, a long hall opened. There were three doors, all closed, but I decided not to check them. Instead, I went up the last, shorter and narrower staircase—leading, I assumed, up to the attic. As far as I could tell, there was either no door or the doorway was open: I could see the dark shape of a table and the ghostly silhouette of flowers.

A faint scent of roses lingered in the air as I stepped just inside the attic door. I breathed in deeply and inhaled the fragrance, partly for pleasure, but also to regain my normal breathing and to steady my heart. A skylight offered a view of a cloudy night sky. The window on my left provided the only light in the room. I made out the silhouette of large objects in the sparsely furnished room—a bed, an armchair, three bookcases and a desk.

As I made my way in the dark, I began to think that I had made a mistake—that perhaps the noise had come from the floor below. Out of the corner of my right eye, I saw a shadow move. With my finger on the trigger ready to fire, I turned quickly towards it. Two dark reflections of myself holding the gun stared back at me an instant later, and I realized I was facing the twin mirrors on a large armoire.

"The wardrobe. Black Widow's wardrobe," I said under my breath.

It was large enough to hide someone inside. I approached it cautiously. I grabbed the door handle, but I remembered something I had read in Celia Howard's book: After her husband's murder, the police said, Licia Lecuona had climbed into the wardrobe when she saw their armed approach. For an instant, I toyed with the idea of putting my weapon away before pulling the door open, but I decided against it. I flung one door open, then the other, and pushed aside the garments hanging in it. No one was there. Curiosity egging me on, I took out my flashlight and pointed its beam on the dresses in the wardrobe, stopping at a long white lace wedding dress with glittering embroidery.

I pulled out the gown just as I heard a rustling of clothes behind me. My back stiffened. Fear shot up my spine as I heard a woman say, "Put it back." I cursed my carelessness inwardly, but I didn't move. Sensing my hesitation, she commanded, "Now."

"Licia Lecuona?" I asked as I put the gown back on the rack.

"Put the flashlight on the floor, then turn around slowly," she said.

"Michael Cisneros sent me. My name is Gloria Damasco."

I put the flashlight down. As unobtrusively as I could, I slid the .38 between my belt and waist, then turned around to face her. She was standing by the door with her back to the window. All I could make out was her sheer long-sleeved white nightgown, glowing in the semi-darkness, and the silhouette of her body within it. She raised one of her arms slightly, and for an instant she looked like a giant, wingless firefly.

Reaching out to the switch by the door, she turned on the light. She had her left arm in a sling, but no weapon in her right hand. Still, I made no move to approach her. Not saying a word, she looked me over. I could see a glimmer of recognition in her eyes as she asked, "May I see your identification?" She walked towards me until she was at arm's length. I handed her my driver's license, but held on to my P.I. card.

"Gloria Inés Damasco," she read aloud. "Damasco is an unusual last name. Your husband's?" she asked, looking in my eyes.

"Uh-huh," I replied.

"Where is your husband now?"

"He died four years ago."

"It's hard for a woman to get rid of a husband's name," she said, handing me back my license. "Even after she kills him." She looked straight at me, a hint of a smile on her lips.

"How is your shoulder?"

"Healing. Quite a coincidence that you were there when I got . . . hurt."

"Isn't it?" I said. I wanted to ask her why she was being so reckless with her life or why she was so determined to die. "Why did you leave the front door unlocked just now?" I asked instead.

"That's not really what you want to ask," she replied, narrowing her eyes. "Don't worry. Everything is under control."

She seemed as poised and self-possessed as that first time I saw her at the bakery cafe, on the Day of the Dead. I picked up my flashlight and turned it off.

Moving towards the wardrobe and me, she said, "You seem to be interested in my wedding dress. I'll show it to you." She pulled the dress off the rack with her right hand.

"It's a beautiful gown," I remarked, as I saw the faded blood stains on its upper skirt. "It was your grandmother's wedding gown, wasn't it?"

Licia gave me an inquisitive look.

I said, "I read Celia Howard's *The Wardrobe*."

"Ah, yes. Then you know the story of Black Widow." I detected a bit of sarcasm in her voice. Putting the gown back on the rack, she pulled out another, a long sky-blue silk dress. Looking at it closely, she said, "You have an advantage over me. I know very little about you, except that you're 'a very good detective, caring and compassionate, and very smart,' as Michael put it. It's always dangerous for a woman to be smart."

She signaled for me to walk to the window, then she turned off the light and joined me there. "It's easier to talk about one's life in the dark, before an open window."

"I suppose," I answered.

For a while, we stood in silence. Then she began to ask me questions. If it had not been for her interest in my zodiac sign and other, similar questions, I would have felt as if I were at a typical job interview. She seemed very interested in Tania, and I had no trouble telling her about my daughter's accomplishments. At last she asked about my profession. Then, apparently satisfied with my answers, she finally said, "We can go downstairs now."

With my hand on the butt of my gun, I followed her to the hall below. She opened one of the doors. Through the large bay window, I saw the top of the old hospital's twin towers. My gaze slid down the towers, the facade of the building and the long staircase leading to it. The dream-vision of the acrobat running up a long staircase flashed through my mind, and I wondered as I walked into the room if I was at the place where my visions would start to become real.

"This will be your room," she said and turned on the light.

It was a sparsely furnished room—an oak double bed with matching nightstands on each side and a large dresser, a desk and chair, an armchair next to a lamp table, and tall bookcases lining one of the walls. On one of the nightstands, I saw a phone and an intercom. A half-open door showed a closet. A second door, opposite the closet, presumably opened to either a bathroom or another bedroom.

"Michael indicated that you'd be spending the night—maybe many nights—here," Licia said, heading towards the door opposite the closet and opening it. She added, "We'll be sharing the bathroom, which connects this room with mine." She turned to face me, then asked, "Do you have any luggage?"

"It's in my car," I answered. "I'll get it as soon as—"

"That won't be necessary," Licia interjected. She walked to one of the nightstands and pressed a button on the intercom. "Carmelo, would you come up, please?"

Trying not to betray my irritation, I asked, "Has he been in the house all along?"

"Yes, he has." She must have sensed my annoyance, for she said, "I apologize for this charade, but I had to be sure you're suited for this job."

"I see," I said. "What's his role in all this?"

"He's not my bodyguard, if that's what you're asking. Michael hired Carmelo years ago to live in the house and take care of the grounds. Occasionally he also drives me where I need to go. Bernardina takes care of the house. She's a more recent arrival, but no less important than him."

A moment later, Carmelo rapped softly on the bedroom door. He was a rather short, stout man, with jet-black straight hair, high cheekbones, and small eyes.

"Please bring Mrs. Damasco's bags," she told him. Turning to me, she said, "Your car keys, please."

"It's the silver Volvo in front of the house," I said to him in Spanish as I handed him my keyring. He bowed, took the keys, and left the room.

"He's from Chiapas. Bernardina is from a village on the Gulf coast, near Coatzacoalcos," she explained. "Coatzacoalcos is a very important port now, near the village where I was first born."

Not sure that I'd heard her right, I asked, "Where you were *first* born? I thought you were an Oakland native."

A gentle smile lit her face. "There'll be plenty of time for explanations. I'm sure you want to unpack and freshen up. When you're ready, join us downstairs for supper. By the way, Carmelo and Bernardina join me at the dinner table every night."

Her hand on the doorknob, she said, "Carmelo will show you how the alarm system works. Feel free to check any room in the house. My life—as you already know—is an open book." She smiled and closed the door quietly behind her.

EIGHTEEN
A Tiny Hope Chest

Two tall bookcases in Licia's reading room, now my room, contained a large alphabetized collection of Chicana poetry books, from Ana Castillo to Bernice Zamora, including the three poetry collections my friend Luisa Cortez had published in her lifetime. But Licia had chapbooks by poets I had not known even existed.

The other bookcases contained volumes on Mexico, from pre-Conquest to modern history, ethnography, geography, and folklore to literature and other fine arts. Each shelf was labeled according to the category. One shelf, labeled MARINA, caught my attention as much for the subject as for the sparsity of books on it.

I wondered how Licia had managed to acquire some of those books from prison. Perhaps through Lester, or bookstores and bookfinders. She had certainly had the resources. I was about to pull out a loose-leaf anthology of essays on Malinche when my cell phone rang.

"Didn't you get my message?" my mother asked.

"No, I haven't checked my messages yet. What did you want to tell me?"

"Nina and I went to the Chicano Studies Library at UC Berkeley. I didn't know so many Chicana writers and poets were interested in Malinche. Anyway, the librarian there gave us copies of some essays by professors, Cypes and Del Castillo. The librarian also told us to talk to Professor Norma Alarcón, who told us that Malinche died more or less at the age of twenty-four, perhaps during a smallpox epidemic that swept through Mexico in 1527. But no one knows for sure how and when Malinche died. At any rate, Malinche's daughter by Jaramillo, María Jaramillo Tenepal, was only a year old when her mother died. Jaramillo remarried a short time after that, to a Spanish woman. He wanted his children from the second marriage to inherit the lands and palaces Cortés had given Malinche, so he took everything away from María."

"So mother and daughter suffered the same fate."

"Yep," my mother said. "Pretty sad. At any rate, Nina and I will continue our search, and we'll let you know if we come across any other information."

"I don't think that'll be necessary," I said. "Obviously, Rosa Catalino made up that story about the connection between Licia and Malinche. For a reason, of course. Now, I have to find out what her reason is."

"Uh, I don't think I can stop now. Nina won't let me," my mother warned. "My *comadre* has caught the fever. She's fascinated with the story of Malinche."

A while later, I went downstairs to join Licia, Carmelo, and Bernardina for dinner.

Dinner turned out to be delightful. Still more enjoyable was the conversation; Bernardina was not only an excellent cook but an entertaining storyteller. Before moving to Mexico City to look for work, she had always lived in a small village near the Veracruz-Tabasco border, a place where the oral tradition was still alive and going strong. Her small village, near the Port of Coatzacoalcos— "where rivers do not pour gently into the restless Gulf of Mexico and summer storms rage all night long," as Licia had put it—was also the place that Licia claimed to be her true place of birth.

Licia listened attentively to Bernardina's stories, as did Carmelo. Carmelo remained silent for the most part. From time to time, Licia contributed a detail or a bit of information the housekeeper overlooked; I gathered that she had heard the stories many times before. Once in a while, she smiled and closed her eyes.

After the storytelling session, Licia retired to her room while Carmelo showed me how the security system worked. We made sure all entrances and windows were locked. Carmelo explained only what was necessary, ignoring all of my questions concerning the attempt on Licia's life or the more recent break-in.

After Carmelo and Bernardina went to bed, I walked around the house in the dark, trying to familiarize myself with my surroundings. Upstairs again, I called Rafael. Dora Saldaña had not shown up. But he assured me that he could take the next day off from school to continue the surveillance of Dora's house.

Hoping to gain an insight into Licia's mind and heart, I perused her collection of books on Malinche. I pulled out the volume of essays. Still smelling of fresh ink, it had untattered covers and lacked the name of the publisher, so I surmised that someone had compiled it for her. I soon realized that some modern-day Chicanas had taken up the task of revising Malinche's history and clearing her name.

Reconstructing Malinche's life accurately had to be quite a difficult task, if not impossible. All the available information on her, complimentary or not, had been provided by men, from Bernal Díaz and other witnesses during the conquest, to López Gómara, Hernán Cortés's biographer. Many had quite an historic ax to grind with Malinche.

I surmised that Chicana scholars and writers aimed at creating a new and more positive view of La Malinche. In doing so, they hoped to give Mexicanas and Chicanas a better sense of themselves, not as *las hijas de la chingada*—the Indian woman violated and subjugated by the conqueror—but as *las hijas de la Malinche*—the daughters of an intelligent woman who had exercised the options available to her and chose her own destiny.

My mind was reaching the point of overload. I turned off the light, lay down, and closed my eyes. Close to the house, Cleo and Chaka, the neighbor's dogs, barked every so often. Farther away, an ambulance wailed increasingly louder as it approached Highland's emergency ward. With difficulty, I drifted into a fitful sleep, only to be startled out of slumber by a noise.

I picked up my flashlight and gun and went into the bathroom. Opening the door to Licia's bedroom slightly, I saw that her bed was empty.

Following my intuition, I went upstairs to the attic. The door was ajar, and I could see the flickering of a candle. I heard a door snapping open, then some kind of grating noise.

With my back against the wall to support myself, I could see inside the room. The doors to the wardrobe were fully open. Licia was crouched over a small, flat Olinalá lacquer chest. From it she pulled out a thin, dark book, like an old savings passbook. When she also took out an air ticket envelope, I realized that the book might be a passport. It had to be a fake one; Michael Cisneros had told me she had asked him to obtain a legal passport for her. She put both objects back into the chest and closed its lid.

As she lifted it, she moved closer to the wardrobe, obstructing my view. An instant later, I heard the same grating sound as before, and I realized that the wardrobe had a secret compartment. *What else does she keep in the chest?* I wondered, as I quietly moved down the stairs.

Back in my room, I quickly closed the door. A few minutes later, I heard Licia's door open and close.

A half-hour later, I opened the door to her room and listened for her breathing. Then I went in to check on her.

She was lying in bed with her back to me, fast asleep. The curtains in her room were not drawn, and some light trickled in. When I got closer to her bed, I noticed a glass of water and a vial of pills on her nighttable. She didn't even stir in bed when I inadvertently knocked the vial over. As I rearranged things on the table, a tiny glint of light hit my pupils. I located its source half-hidden under one of Licia's pillows: a knife.

I went back to my room and looked at the clock; it was 3:10 in the morning. Leaving the hall door to my room open, I went back to bed, but I couldn't regain sleep. An hour had passed when I heard creaking noises again: Someone was walking up the stairs. I sat up in bed and pulled out my gun. Anyone trying to reach Licia's room would have to go past my door or go through my room. I rose and took a position next to the hall door. I closed my eyes, took a breath and held it, and listened intently. An instant later, I heard the door to the attic open. I exhaled and stuck my head out.

The hallway was clear. I had begun to make my way down the hall when I saw another shadow step onto the landing. I was almost sure it was Carmelo. I thought of calling out his name but decided against it.

As I was going up the stairs to the attic, I saw the light go on, then I heard Carmelo's and Bernardina's muffled voices. They seemed to be arguing. Bernardina's tone turned to a pleading murmur a moment later.

Holding the gun with both hands, I pushed the door gently with my foot and stepped into the room. Bernardina, standing in front of the open wardrobe, saw me first and let out a soft cry. I could see the terror in her eyes. Carmelo, who was standing with his back to me, turned around completely, took two slow steps back until he was standing beside Bernardina. He didn't seem even slightly fazed by the gun being pointed at him.

"What's going on here?" I asked with a raspy voice, then cleared my throat.

"Nothing," Carmelo answered. His face was expressionless. "We both heard noises up here and came to see what was going on."

"I see," I said, looking around. Other than the open wardrobe, nothing seemed disturbed. "Did you think someone was hiding in the wardrobe?" I asked, looking directly at Bernardina.

She shook her head, then began to sob.

"Do you always send a woman to check a place where someone might be hiding?" I asked Carmelo.

He tensed up. His eyes narrowed as he looked at me, but he said nothing.

"Why don't you go downstairs?" I told Bernardina.

Not taking her eyes off the gun, she moved cautiously towards the door, then ran down the stairs.

"I think you owe me an explanation," I told Carmelo.

I pulled up a chair, sat down, and pointed at another chair a little farther away. He hesitated but finally sat down. He stared at the gun without blinking or moving a muscle, almost as if in a trance. For the first time I sensed in him the terror that he was trying so hard to supress. I lowered my gun. He let out a sigh of relief.

"I gather you've stared at death before," I said. "Where? When?"

"In my village in Guatemala, a few miles from the border with Chiapas. I was ten years old when the government soldiers rode into my village for the first time. They killed half the population. When I was fifteen, they came back. They wanted to take all the teen-aged boys to join the army. Many of them refused and were shot. But that time I wasn't among them. Earlier that evening, I had gone to a neighboring village to see my girlfriend. So I wasn't at home when the soldiers arrived. My parents knew that the soldiers would kill me if they ever found me, so they sent me to Mexico, where I lived for a few years. Through the American Friends, I met some people who were working with the sanctuary program. They brought me over to Oakland and introduced me to Mr. Cisneros. He gave me a job. During the Immigration Amnesty Program, I was able to get my green card. When Mr. Cisneros asked me to move to this house, I agreed."

"What happened to your parents?"

"They're dead. There was a second raid on my village a few months after I left. No one survived the attack."

"I'm very sorry," I said. "Doesn't it bother you to live in a house with a woman who killed her husband?"

"I'm not one to throw the first stone. Guatemalan jails are full of people who've had to kill to defend themselves from a violent agressor. Who's to say who's guilty?"

"I guess you're right," I said. "When did Michael—Mr. Cisneros—hire Bernardina?"

"He didn't. *La señora* Licia hired her. I think Bernardina was recommended by a woman *la señora* knows, someone she met in prison and who was very good to her."

"Do you happen to know this woman's name?"

"Yes. Her name is Rosa. That's all I know."

"So, what was Bernardina doing in the attic?"

"I really can't tell you because I don't know. She said she heard some noise and came to check it out."

"Did she think there were rats in the wardrobe?" I asked.

"My question, too," he said. For the first time, Carmelo smiled.

"Has she done anything like this before?"

"I don't think so."

"Now that we're aware of her *curiosity*, let's keep an eye on her. Perhaps it's better if we don't tell Licia anything about this for the time being."

Carmelo agreed with a nod.

"I'm assuming you know that someone is trying to kill Licia," I said.

"Yes." He seemed mortified. "I should have been with her last Friday."

"Why weren't you?"

"She didn't say she was going to the Procession of the Dead. She claimed she had a headache and went to bed early. I didn't know she'd been out until she came home—wounded. Bernardina and I tried our best to take care of her. I asked her about it, but she told me to forget it'd happened."

"Do you have any idea who's trying to kill her? Any idea at all?"

"I don't. I'm sorry."

"Do you know who Dora Saldaña is?"

"No, I don't. Who is she?"

"A private investigator. She was following you the night of the attempted burglary," I explained.

"Do you think she's behind all this?"

"I don't know. I have someone watching her house, just in case."

"Let me know what I can do to help."

"Do you trust me, then?"

"Mr. Cisneros trusts you, and that's good enough for me," he replied and got up. Saying goodnight, he left.

For a while, I stood in front of the open wardrobe, unable to decide whether I should look into Licia's secrets. I seemed to have no choice if I was to keep her out of harm's way. I was getting ready to look for the mechanism to the secret compartment when I heard Carmelo say behind me, "Come quickly. There's something you should see."

NINETEEN
The Jade-eyed God

Carmelo led me and a reluctant, teary-eyed Bernardina through the kitchen to the basement, which was filled with old furniture. Below a small window, there were also a washer and dryer.

Holding onto Bernardina with one hand, he said, "She was getting ready to leave with this. It was hidden behind that dresser." He picked up a dark green knapsack and handed it to me.

I set it down on the washer and unzipped it. I reached in and took out some small zip-lock plastic bags with crushed, dry leaves in them: marijuana. Some larger bags were full of mushrooms. A few others were filled with small chunks of some kind of cactus.

On the bottom there was a small package, wrapped in banana leaves and tied with a string. I unwrapped it and found a piece of jewelry about the size of an open palm. It was a profiled head and face, made of turquoise. A slanted jade eye stared from beneath an arched, silver-inlaid brow and elaborate plumed headdress. I didn't know much about pre-Columbian art, but it looked genuine.

"Where did you get this?" I asked Bernardina.

She started to cry again.

"You're already in a lot of trouble. We could turn this bag over to the police. You'd go to jail. Please, tell us where you got all these," Carmelo told her.

"I already know that Rosa went to jail because she was smuggling drugs over the border," I said. "She probably wants you to keep them here in case the police search her house."

She began to tremble and shake her head.

Carmelo put his arm around her shoulder. *"Dinos de qué tienes miedo,*" he said in a reassuring tone. Tell us what you are so afraid of.

Switching to Spanish, Bernardina explained that she didn't have a green card. Rosa had promised to help her get one, but had threatened to report her to immigration if Bernardina didn't do as she was told.

Bernardina began to sob again. "I can't go back to Mexico. I only have an uncle who lives in Coyoacán but he can't protect me from . . . I was a maid to a rich family in Mexico City. My *patrón* raped me and I . . ." She broke down and fell to her knees, sobbing.

"It's okay. We won't call the *Migra* on you. But what does Rosa want from you . . . other than your keeping these drugs for her?"

"Rosa wants some things Licia has—things that Licia took from her when they were in prison." She wiped her eyes with the back of her hand.

"What *things?*"

"Some papers and photos. Rosa told me to find those papers. I was looking for them upstairs," she said, looking at Carmelo.

Rosa had told me only half the truth about her dispute with Licia—who had indeed taken those documents. I mentally moved Rosa to the top of the suspect list again.

"How did you know where to look?" I asked.

"I didn't know. But I had looked everywhere else."

"Did Rosa tell you why she wants those papers and photos?"

"She just said that a man is going to pay a lot of money for them. But this man is going away soon. So she needs to have those papers right away. She said that I can finally get my green card, and she can move to Mexico and never worry about money again."

"What are you supposed to do with these?" I asked, pointing at the plastic bags and the jewelry.

"Take them to her."

"When and where?"

"Tomorrow. She's going to call me and tell me where to take

them," she said.

"Tomorrow? You mean today. It's already Friday," Carmelo stated. Bernardina agreed with a nod.

"Are you supposed to deliver the papers she wants, too?" She nodded again.

"Okay. We'll wait for her phone call. I'll take it from there," I said. "We'll help you, but you have to promise you'll do as we tell you." When she agreed, I told her to go back to bed.

After Bernardina left, Carmelo asked, "Are you sure we can trust her?"

"We have no choice," I answered. "Keep your eyes and ears open. I'll keep this bag in my room."

I went upstairs, slid the knapsack under my bed, and went into Licia's room to check on her. She was still sound asleep. At least one of us was getting some rest.

I went up to the attic once more. I had decided not to hide, so I turned on the light and began to look for the mechanism that opened the secret compartment in Licia's wardrobe, and found it quickly.

I took out the wooden chest, set it on a table, and opened it. The passport was for Licia but had expired fifteen years earlier. The airline ticket was issued to her for travel on the red-eye flight to Mexico City, Sunday, November 12. In the same envelope I also found her birth certificate. According to that document, she had indeed been born in Mexico, but not Coatzacoalcos, as she claimed. She had been born in a hospital in Coyoacán.

I looked back in the lacquer box, and found a second birth certificate. It, too, was in Spanish. As far as I could tell, it registered the birth of a baby girl, Elena Tomasa Briones Castillo, born at that same hospital twenty years *before* Licia. Her mother? Making a mental note to ask Michael Cisneros about it, I went back to what was left in the box.

Underneath the passport, clipped to a folded note, were three color photographs. The first showed a man's hands grasping a small, black urn. The back of one hand, wrapped around the artifact, bore the long line of a scar that ran from the groove between his thumb and index finger to his wrist. I remembered seeing that scar on Professor Legorreta's hand when he pushed his wife Isabela away. The second snap showed the outside of a post office and a man—who looked like the professor—entering the building. The third clearly showed Legorreta and his children, Inés and Martín, outside their home in Livermore.

I unfolded the note attached to the photographs. Dated April 15, 1990, it was addressed to Rosa Catalino at the California Correctional Institution for Women.

> *Dear Mother,*
> *Don't you just love it? The business is going well. El profesor says he'll come through as he promised. I hope to visit you during the Memorial Day weekend. I'll bring the bank statements to show you how well the business is doing.*

I pondered the photos and note. These were clearly Rosa's "misplaced" papers. As to the connection between Legorreta and Rosa Catalino, I didn't have a complete picture yet. But I surmised that he had probably been using Rosa to smuggle pre-Columbian artifacts across the border. It occurred to me that the spiritualist might be blackmailing the professor. If nothing else, his professional reputation was at stake. He would surely pay to protect it. But how did Licia fit in the picture? Did Legorreta know that Licia had these incriminating documents?

No, I concluded: Rosa's blackmailing scheme worked only if the professor believed she still had them in her possession. Otherwise, why force Bernardina to get them for her?

I put the photos next to the ticket and passport on the table, and reached into the box for the last items in it. My confusion increased as I carefully unfolded wornout, yellowing photostats of two documents, and a partial text of a typewritten note:

> The professor and his wife are very pleased and we all can expect payment soon. I'll be in touch.

There was no signature, but judging by the black lines running across, both above and below the excerpt, I was sure that someone had gone to some trouble to block out the rest of the letter.

Turning my attention to the other two photostats, I saw that they were death certificates. Both were dated November 2, 1972. They recorded the deaths of two stillborn twin infants, a boy and a girl, delivered by Caesarean section on Wednesday, November 1, 1972, at 6:01 a.m. and 6:04 a.m. respectively. Listed as the babies' parents were Licia Román Lecuona and Peter Percy Lecuona, the latter marked as "deceased." The second document must have been handled quite a bit, or a poor copy made of it, for, without the aid of a magnifying glass I was unable to make out most of the data.

I sat back in the armchair, holding the photostats. Time and again I arrived at the same conclusion: In all likelihood, Inés and Martín Legorreta were Licia's children. Who had helped the Legorretas abduct the babies? Who had arranged for the death certificates and then obtained fake birth certificates? The first suspect inevitably was the obstetrician who had delivered them, aided perhaps by others at the prison. Most likely, a lawyer had seen to filing the necessary paperwork. I wrote down the name of the obstetrician, still legible in the first certificate. I would have to locate his whereabouts, then see where it all led.

But how had the birth certificates come into Licia's hands? From Dora Saldaña? Lester Zamora? Had Licia threatened to expose the Legorretas? Fearing exposure and prosecution, were they now trying to kill her?

I thought of leaving the box on the table and the wardrobe open to force the issue. But Bernardina was still in the house, and she could easily take them. For a moment I even considered that possibility: If Bernardina took the papers to Rosa Catalino and she sold them to the Legorretas, there would no longer be a reason for them to kill Licia. But that would obliterate any possibility that Licia could ever be reunited with her children. I had the feeling that this tiny hope was all that was keeping Licia Lecuona alive. I put the contents back in the chest, and the chest in the wardrobe.

Back in my room, I pulled out the books on Pre-Columbian art. Looking for something similar to the turquoise and jewelry piece in the knapsack, I began to flip through the pages. At last, I found an illustration of a stone rubbing that resembled the piece. I took the jewel out. It was almost an exact replica: the ancient god, Tepoztecatl. According to the book, the deity was worshipped by the Tepozteca people in a small town that still stood at the foot of the Ajusco sierra, in the state of Morelos. In pre-Conquest times, Tepoztecatl had presided over birthday celebrations and weddings, and over funeral rites. He was the ancient god of *pulque*, the fermented juice of the agave plant.

Reaching again to the bookshelves, I searched in an atlas of Mexico for a map of the Morelos region.

The Ajusco mountain range rimmed an eight-shaped valley. One of the halves was the Valley of Cuauhnahuac, which had been renamed Cuernavaca after the conquest. Hernán Cortés had erected his summer palace in Cuernavaca and had lived there with his indispensable Malinche, waiting for the opportunity to march on the ancient capital of the Aztec empire. Only a short distance from Cuernavaca was Tepoztlan, a small town where the slanted jade-eyed god's people lived.

And Celia Howard had mentioned that the Lecuonas had moved to Cuernavaca shortly after Licia was convicted of killing their son Peter.

I'd hardly had any sleep and I was beginning to feel giddy. I closed the atlas, returned the jewel to the knapsack and the books to their shelves. I turned off the light and pulled the covers over my exhausted body. For a long time my mind refused to surrender to slumber, and I pondered questions to which I had no answers yet.

TWENTY
Unborn Memory

My mental alarm clock rang at six forty-five in the morning. I'd hardly opened my eyes when my cellular phone rang. Rafael was at the other end. "Ms. Saldaña's been home all night, but she just now came out and put something in the trunk of her car. She's probably going somewhere. Want me to follow her?"

"Yes, but just long enough for me to get to you. I'll take it from there. I don't want you to miss school. Did you get any sleep?"

"Yeah, some. Don't worry. I'm okay," Rafael answered. "Hey, she's leaving. Get ready. I'll call you."

I got up, checked on Licia (still asleep), showered, and dressed. I slid the .38 into my handbag, picked up the cell phone, then went downstairs.

Carmelo greeted me with a smile. Bernardina gave me a couple of furtive glances as she handed me the coffee I'd asked for and went back to the kitchen immediately.

"I'm going out," I told Carmelo. "I have to talk to Dora Saldaña. Do you remember I told you about her last night?"

"I remember. She's the other P.I., the one who was following us the night of the break-in."

"That's her. I've located her and I'd like to have a talk with her." I looked at my watch. Carmelo looked at his. "It's seven-ten right now. I'll be back by ten o'clock at the latest. If anything happens, call me at this number." I handed him a slip of paper with my cell phone number.

I went down to my car to wait for Rafael's call. I cupped my hands over my eyes and kept them open until the moist warmth began to sooth them. Inadvertently, I closed my eyes and went into a deep sleep. When the phone rang again fifteen minutes later, I was amazed at how rested I felt. I pressed the talk button.

"She just got off the freeway and is heading towards the Maxwell Park area. Do you know where that is?"

I started my car as I replied, "Indeed I do. I think I know where she's going, too."

Since I was traveling east on I-580 in the opposite direction of the commute traffic, I was able to get to Lester Zamora's house fast. The black Taurus was parked a few feet down the street from the house when I got there. Rafael's car was right behind it.

"Give me ten minutes. If you don't hear any gunfire, go home," I joked.

"You know I can't do that," Rafael answered. "I'll walk you to the door. At least, they'll know you're not alone."

Lester opened the door. If he was surprised to see me at his doorstep, he didn't show it.

"Good morning," he greeted me. "I see you brought the cavalry with you," he said when he saw Rafael. "Come in, both of you. You might as well join us. It's obvious you both can use a cup of my industrial-strength Java."

"I'm in need of an explanation," I said, "not coffee."

"We'll get to that in due time. But, first, I want you to meet a colleague of yours," he replied, opening the door wide. Rafael and I stepped in.

"Dora Saldaña," I said, as I looked at the tall Chicana, dressed in a mock-turtle neck sweater, mid-length wool skirt, and cowboy boots. She was standing in the middle of the living room with her legs apart, one of her arms behind her and the other hanging tensely along her torso and hip, with her hand hidden in a fold of her skirt. I suspected that hand was holding a weapon, and her eyes told me she could use it. I stood in place and held her stare. As Lester made the introductions, she put the gun on the table.

"That's better," Lester said, with a sigh of relief. He wiped his forehead with the back of his hand. "Now, we can talk."

"Will you be okay, Gloria?" Rafael asked.

"Yes. Go on or you'll be late. I'll call you at home later.

Thanks."

"If I don't hear from you—" Rafael began.

"Don't worry, son. She'll call you," Lester interjected and walked him to the door.

"Nice little stunt you pulled the other night," Dora said.

"Thanks. You owe me a fender," I replied.

Lester came back in and signaled for Dora and me to follow him to the dining room. Then, he went into the kitchen and came out carrying a pot of steaming coffee and *pan dulce*.

"Would you mind telling me what this is all about?" I asked Lester, throwing a glance at Dora. "She was outside Licia's house at the time of the break-in and she's been following me ever since."

"After you left the other night, I immediately called Dora and asked her to get over to Licia's house and keep an eye on her," he answered. "It's simple. Not that I don't trust you, but I wanted to make sure you were who you said."

"Nothing simple about all this, since she's also done some work for Licia. And you knew about it," I said. Every so often, I looked at Dora, who sipped her coffee indifferently.

"What do *you* have to say about it?" I at last asked her directly.

She looked at Lester. After he nodded, she said, "It's true. Some years ago, I did look into a matter for Licia Lecuona, at Mr. Zamora's request."

"What matter?"

"Mrs. Lecuona wanted to find out if her baby daughter had really died," she said.

"Did she?"

"No. The baby didn't die. She was adopted." Lester answered this time.

"Correction," Dora said, with indignation in her voice. "The babies—two of them—were stolen and sold."

"Were the Legorretas and the Lecuonas behind their abduction and illegal adoption?"

Both Lester and Dora gave me a puzzled look.

"Inés and Martín Legorreta are twins, about eighteen years old."

When he realized I already knew part of the story, he smiled and said, "I see you've been busy since we last talked. What else do you know?"

"I'd like to hear what you know first," I said to Dora.

"We don't know for sure that either the Legorretas or the Lecuonas are behind this fraudulent adoption. But we've suspected as much," Lester said to me.

"For something like this to happen, there had to be quite a few people involved," I remarked.

Dora stirred in her chair. "Quite a few people. But both the physician who delivered the babies and the prison nurse who assisted died some years back, under highly suspicious circumstances. The doctor, who had no history of alcoholism, was killed after he hit a telephone post while DUI. Two years later, the nurse was run down by an unknown driver in a supermarket parking lot, while she was carrying her groceries out to her car. And then, that shyster J. A. Hardwood fled the country when the feds got too close for comfort. His files were confiscated and sealed. Dead end!"

"That's all fine," I said. "But, who told you that the doctor and nurse were involved to begin with?"

"Licia did," both answered in unison.

For the next fifteen minutes, I listened attentively to Dora's and Lester's haphazard account of their conversations with Licia. A prison guard—a woman about to retire and who had knowledge of the scheme—had felt guilty and had told Licia that she had given birth to not one but two babies. Licia, who had been given general anesthesia during the C-section, had no idea whether the guard was telling the truth, but she knew the name of the obstetrician and his nurse. She had begged Lester to try to find out who had adopted her babies, and Lester in turn hired Dora to look into the guard's claim.

During her investigation, Dora found out that the obstetrician was dead, but she went to see his wife, hoping that she'd kept her husband's records. The doctor's wife apparently had no idea what her husband had done, and wanting to clear his name, the woman had let Dora look at the records.

Dora found two photostats of the babies' death certificates. She also came across a note to the obstetrician from "that monster Hardwood," stating that he had obtained false birth certificates for the infants. In that note, the attorney also told the doctor they all could expect payment soon, as "the professor and his wife" were "very pleased" with their performance.

"Peter Lecuona had only one sister, Isabela Lecuona Legorreta. She was married to a professor. At the time, they had no children. Then suddenly they did. The twins fit the profile to a T," Dora said.

"How much does Licia know?" I asked.

"When Dora came to me with all this information, I told Licia that the prison guard was probably right," Lester said, "but that Hardwood's files had been sealed. Since then I've regretted having told her anything. She was grief-stricken and went on a fast, hardly eating anything for a long time. Twice, she was taken to the prison infirmary after she passed out. Little by little, she seemed to get over her grief. Then, about two years ago, she seemed full of life and even cheerful. She started telling me about Rosa Catalino and how much this woman had helped her understand what had happened to her. But she didn't talk about her babies again, that is, until the day after she was released from prison."

"Wait. Go back. Rosa Catalino knew about the adoption?" I asked.

"I'm not sure Licia told her about it," Lester replied. "Why? Is that woman involved?"

"I'm not sure at this point. But Rosa certainly knows Legorreta. She's possibly even done business with him."

Dora cursed under her breath. "Do you want me to do anything about this?" Dora asked Lester.

"First let's see what happens here today," he answered. "Is there anything else *you'd* care to share with us?" he asked me.

"Not for the time being. But I'd like to know what happened the day Licia was released from prison."

"I picked her up from the prison. Almost as soon as we got in the car, she began to ask me—to beg me—to hire someone to break into the FBI's evidence room in San Francisco to steal Hardwood's files." Lester paused briefly. "When I said I wouldn't do it, she said nothing. She just looked at me and said, 'You've been a good friend, my only friend. Thank you.' And, somehow, I knew she was saying goodbye, that I would not see her again."

Lester let out a long sigh, overcome with sorrow. Dora swallowed hard. It seemed useless, but I reached out to Lester and held his hand. He attempted a smile. Letting go of my hand, he took out his handkerchief and wiped the moisture around his eyes. "When you came to see me, I suspected Licia hadn't left matters alone. So I asked Dora to keep an eye on her, and on you."

"Why on me? I didn't know any more than I told you."

"But I knew you were determined to find out," he answered. "I didn't really know if you had a client. And . . . Actually, I was going to suggest to both of you that you work together."

At first, Dora and I were dumbstruck. Then, both of us voiced our respective protests. Dora worked alone. I already had a partner and a client. We wouldn't get along.

"But you both share a common goal: to keep Licia alive," Lester pointed out. "Listen, Gloria, we already know you moved into Licia's house. This is all guesswork, but I'm assuming you had to hire the young man who was with you to watch Dora's house. Obviously, you can't be everywhere at once."

Without meaning to do it, I tilted my head and nodded. Still, I wasn't sure that Michael Cisneros would agree to using two detectives.

"I may have to clear that with my client," I said. "I don't think he'd be willing to pay her fee as well."

"That shouldn't be a problem. I can take care of it."

Lester turned to Dora and said, "You know Gloria went to see the spiritualist, but you don't know what transpired at her house.

Unless Gloria tells you about the goings-on at Licia's, you have no way of knowing. How can you make any progress from now on without Gloria's help?" Dora showed no sign of agreeing to his request. "Of course, you might just want to call it quits."

Dora rose to her full five-feet-nine. Although her abundant long hair was tied back, she brushed some invisible strands back in a gesture of defiance. "I never quit. People say many things about me, that I'm a *cabrona*, that I would use my mother and grandmother, and even my dog, to get the work done, that I'm a brazen, pushy, and opinionated bitch. And it's all true. I don't take shit from no one. But two things they'll never say, that I'm stupid or a quitter."

Lester smiled. I couldn't help a chuckle.

Fuming, Dora said, "You find me comical?"

"No," I said. "I've also used my mother and her *comadre* to do some work for me. I'd accept my dog's help if I had one, too."

"Have you, now," Dora said and snorted noisily.

Laughing, Lester said, "You see? You two have more in common than you think."

"You're a manipulator," Dora said.

"I'm a litigator."

"All right," Dora said, turning to me. "What do you know that I don't?"

"Now we're in business," Lester remarked, helping himself to a croissant. For the next half hour, I gave them a brief account of my experience at Rosa Catalino's house and her belief that Licia was La Malinche's reincarnation, and the spiritualist's claim that to find Licia's would-be murderer I had to find out who had stabbed Malinche. My short visit with the Legorreta family got Lester's and Dora's full attention, as did the events of the night before, which led to the discovery of the pre-Columbian jewelry and the drugs in the knapsack. I talked briefly about the contents of the small chest in Licia's wardrobe.

"Did you know that Licia was actually born in Mexico—Coyoacán to be more precise?" I asked Lester.

"Yes, I know," Lester answered. "Licia told me a long time

ago. Her mother was a Mexican national. She went back to Mexico to have Licia. I guess she wanted to be close to her family at such a time. I'm not sure when Licia became a naturalized U.S. citizen. Why is this important?"

"Not important, I guess. I'm just trying to piece the full picture together here."

"Licia is very smart. Since, as you say, her U.S. passport has expired, she might be planning to use her Mexican birth certificate to enter Mexico legally," Lester offered.

"That might well be the case," I said. I shifted my attention to Dora. "Anything troubling you?"

"Not about the birth certificate. I've been thinking. Since you have to stay close to Licia, let me deliver the knapsack to this Rosa Catalino. I'll get the truth out of her."

I agreed. "By the way," I said, "Do you have a passport?"

"As a matter of fact, I do."

"My client has informed me that Licia may be traveling soon. Knowing what I now know, I think Mexico—the Cuaunahuac Valley in particular—is her destination."

"I have a gun, and I'm always willing to travel," Dora said in jest. I could see she was excited at the prospect.

"To smuggle guns into Mexico is asking for real trouble," I warned. "We'll have to come up with an alternate plan. I think my client has some contacts in Mexico City. Maybe my partner Justin does, too."

Dora and I strategized for her meeting with Rosa Catalino. She also volunteered to keep tabs on the Legorretas, who probably also were getting ready to travel.

During our exchange, Lester had gone into the living room. He sat quietly in what I gathered was his favorite chair, indulging in the view of the misty East Oakland hills. He raised his hand and waved goodbye as I left.

As I got in my car, I wondered if I had made a mistake in confessing to Justin my love for him. I cringed at the thought that I might find myself one day, like Lester Zamora, sitting at home, seeking comfort in the unborn memory of an unrequited love.

TWENTY-ONE
Black Widow's Wardrobe

On my way back to the Victorian, I called Michael Cisneros and told him about the fraudulent adoption of Licia's children and her desire to get them back. I also gave him a brief report on the events at Licia's house the night before. Given the turn of events, he didn't object to my collaboration with Dora Saldaña.

Having done some work for Michael before, I knew he had many business acquaintances in Mexico City as the head of Black Swan International. Talks for an international fair-trade agreement among Mexico, Canada, and the United States were already underway. I had recently read in the newspaper that Cisneros was among a group of Bay Area businessmen who had been asked for their input.

"Do you know anyone in Mexico City who could give us some help if we need it?" I asked.

"What specifically do you have in mind?"

"We need someone who's familiar not only with Mexico City but with the Cuernavaca area as well."

"That can be arranged. Is that all?"

"We could use . . . we can't carry weapons across the Mexican border, so this contact in Mexico City would also have to provide us with some protection."

"I'll see what I can do," he said without hesitation. "I'll be in touch."

When I finally got back to Licia's house, it was past ten o'clock. Rosa Catalino had not called yet, and Licia was taking her daily bath, Carmelo informed me.

"She asked for you. I told you you had to run some errands. She wants you to join her in her room for breakfast. Bernardina's going to take it up soon; she'll knock on your door when it's ready."

"How is Bernardina doing?"

"Still shook up, but she knows we're not going to hurt her or turn her in to the *Migra*," he answered. "How did your meeting go? Any progress?"

"Yes. Dora is going to deliver the knapsack to Rosa. She'll be checking with me later. I'd appreciate it if you answer the phone from now on," I requested. "Is it possible to leave the alarm on for windows and other doors, but keep the front door unarmed?"

"Sure. The way it's set up, we can isolate any part of the house, including the front door."

"I want everything but the front door secured. I don't want any surprises."

Carmelo went to set the alarm. I was tempted to call Justin, but resisted the impulse. I was walking upstairs when my cell phone rang.

"We've got it. We found it!" Nina announced. I didn't get a chance to get a word in from that moment on as she told me about her findings.

"A Mexican historian, who also claims Malinche died of smallpox, made some references to a book by an Otilia Meza. This woman claims that a masked assassin stabbed Malinche thirteen times, outside her house in Mexico City. Thirteen times! Apparently this killer was sent by Cortés and Juan de Jaramillo, Malinche's husband. You see, Cortés was under attack from his many enemies. The *señor conquistador* wasn't just the conqueror of Mexico. He was also quite a ladies' man. When Cortés moved to Coyoacán, he built a house for Malinche a short distance from his hacienda. He even had a chapel built across from her house so she could worship in privacy. But while he lived in his hacienda, he fucked every woman that walked into his house, including two who were mother and daughter. Can you believe it? He had nerve," Nina said vehemently. "*The Great Fornicator*—that's what Mexican historians call him." She laughed.

I laughed, too. "Just the same, what does that have to do with

Malinche's death?"

"Well. Cortés's enemies were trying to bring him to trial for his immoral conduct and for having killed his *first* wife. Of course, what they really wanted was to bring him down and take all his property and land holdings."

"Are you saying that Malinche was also conspiring to bring Cortés down?"

"No. But his enemies were trying to use her. And I guess that even after all she'd done for Cortés, he wasn't so sure of Malinche's loyalty to him. There's something about having all that power that eats at men's good hearts and minds, I tell you."

"What's the name of that book, the one written by Otilia Meza?" I asked as I reached the bookcase in which Licia kept all the books about Malinche.

"Let me see . . ." She paused. I gathered she was looking through her notes. "*Malinalli Tenepal: La gran calumniada.* I guess that means 'The Most Maligned Woman.'"

I looked in the bookcase for the book and found it.

"Good work, Nina," I said. "Thank you."

"*De nada,*" she said. "Believe me, it has been a pleasure. Any time."

Unfortunately, Otilia Meza's biography was in Spanish. Not being used to reading Spanish often, I knew I was going to have to struggle through it. I nonetheless sat down at the reading table in the room and began to skim the last few chapters, reading carefully only those parts that caught my attention. I was engrossed in my reading when I heard a tapping on the bathroom door.

"Come in," I said. I expected Bernardina to walk in and announce that breakfast was ready. Instead, Licia walked gingerly into the room. Since she no longer had her arm in a sling, I gathered she was regaining her use of it. She wasn't wearing any makeup, and her hair was braided, pulled back, and pinned behind her head. Dressed in a white, long cotton sweater and pants, she looked like a model. I marveled at her understated beauty. I couldn't help thinking that if Malinche looked like her, it was no wonder Cortés had found her so attractive.

"May I?" she asked as she reached for the book. Putting her index finger between the pages I was reading, she turned the book over to read the title. "Ah, yes. A most maligned woman, that Malinche," she commented. She looked at me and smiled as she handed the book back to me. Then, she signaled for me to follow her to her room.

The curtains were drawn and sunlight streamed into the large room through the tall bay windows facing the hills in the east. But Bernardina had set our meal on a small table by the windows facing west. In the distance, half of the Bay Bridge, the bay islands, and all of San Francisco were still submerged in a sea of fog.

Licia and I ate in silence. My thoughts gradually shifted to Justin, somewhere in Los Angeles. Why hadn't he tried to get in touch with me? What was he thinking, feeling? I tried to think of something to say to Licia, but a clot of sadness lodged in my throat, impairing all effort to speak.

I was relieved when Licia broke the silence. "People consume only what they have at hand. Such is the case for history, don't you think?" she asked.

"I suppose we believe what historians tell us, if that's what you mean. We would get a rounder view only if all sides were presented. But that's rarely the case."

"Precisely. But even then, people choose to believe what they fancy as the truth," she said. "What do you think the truth is about Malinche?"

I was quiet for a few seconds. "I don't know. I can only tell you what others have said about her. Without her own written testimony, I can only second-guess her reasons for fighting beside Cortés against the Aztecs. I can only speculate on the speculation of others. Not much truth left in that," I finally said. "Perhaps you can tell me about her."

"What makes you think I know any more than you?" she asked.

"I had a talk with Rosa Catalino. she tells me that you believe you're Malinche's reincarnation."

Licia put down her fork, raised her napkin, and with deliberation wiped some invisible morsels of food from her lips.

"Who else have you talked to about me?" she asked, not looking at me.

"Michael Cisneros, of course, and Lester Zamora," I answered. I didn't mention Dora Saldaña or Isabela Legorreta. "Lester cares a great deal for you. And Michael has your welfare in mind. I think you know that. Ever since last Friday night, *I* have *also* been concerned about what's happening to you. How can I not be? Someone tried to kill you that night."

"So," she finally said, "you're not a detective."

"Yes, I am."

"All right. Then tell me, who is trying to kill me?"

"I don't exactly know yet how all the pieces fit together, but Juan Gabriel Legorreta immediately comes to mind as a prime suspect."

Licia didn't say anything. Instead, she closed her eyes. I could see her eyes move rapidly beneath their lids. Her breathing quickened. With her eyes still shut, she began, "I have been called a traitor to my people." She paused again.

"But who were my people? My poor mother, who gave me away to the slave traders because as a woman she could retain her power only through her male child? The slave traders to whom I was only a commodity? My Mayan and Tabascoan masters? The Mexicas who subjugated everyone and went to war for the sole purpose of getting human hearts to appease their gods' wrath? To whom did I owe my loyalty? No. I belonged to no one," she said. "I didn't belong, that was part of my problem. I betrayed no one, except my children."

"How did you . . . did Malinche betray her children?" I asked.

"I thought I was doing the right thing when *mi señor* asked me to let my son live with him. He loved Martín so much. I trusted him with my life, why not my son's? But he gave my son to the care of others. I couldn't even see him or hold him sometimes. They wouldn't let me. Then *mi señor* decided to explore new territory south of Oaxaca. I suppose he wanted to add another victory and offer the Spanish crown the riches of those lands.

Mostly, I think he did it because he was bored. He was a restless man, a man of action, a conqueror. He had to constantly pit himself against an enemy, even if that enemy was only nature itself. That I could understand, but I didn't understand why, for no good reason, he offered me in marriage to Juan de Jaramillo."

"How did you feel about that?" I asked.

"I felt angry and helpless. Jaramillo wasn't even one of his best captains, and he was drunk when we got married. I felt *mi señor* had betrayed me. But I had no choice. If I didn't go along, I would lose everything I had. I had promised myself that I would never be a slave again."

"How did you die Doña Marina? Is it true that Cortés and Jaramillo commissioned your death because you had become a threat to Cortés?"

Beneath their lids, Licia's eyes began to move rapidly again. She was agitated as she replied, "*Mi señor* didn't have me killed. I was no threat to him and he knew it."

"Who, then? Who killed you?"

"I . . . my . . ." Licia began to say, but couldn't or wouldn't complete the sentence. With her eyes still closed, she got up. She reeled back. She stumbled, gesturing in the air as if she were protecting herself from some unknown assailant. Then, she opened her eyes wide. Fear poured out of her pupils, flooding her face, distorting her features. Her mouth opened as if to let out a cry, but no sound came.

She walked quickly to her bed. I pushed my chair back and got up, remembering the knife. I lunged towards the bed, landing on it. But she had already pulled the knife out. Raising it, she struck the pillow twice, missing my arm by a couple of inches.

Terrified, I watched her raise the knife again. The blade became a starburst with the sunlight. Deflected beams struck my retinas, blinding me for a second. I jumped off the bed in the opposite direction and, cautiously, started to circle around it, trying to figure out a way to take the knife away from her. But this time, she didn't strike down. Her hand stayed in midair. She seemed mesmerized, gazing at the shining blade. Slowly, she began to lower her hand, then to turn the knife towards herself. She closed her eyes and threw her head slightly back. Her face was again serene, masked by death's promise of ending grief.

"Don't do it!"

The hand that held the knife began to tremble. "Put it down," I added, softening my voice. I was close enough to grab her arm, but I didn't.

Licia opened her eyes. She stared at me with vacant eyes and took a step back.

"I will help you get your children back," I said. "Please give me the knife."

It dropped to the floor. A stream of tears began to roll down her cheeks. As if she were blind, she stretched out her arm and stumbled towards the door. I stepped out of her way, then followed her. In the hall, she walked faster and faster until she was running up the stairs to the attic, sobbing inconsolably.

As I reached the attic she was already pulling the gowns and dresses off the rack of the wardrobe and throwing them on the floor. She scrambled into the wardrobe and huddled there, her arms around her legs and her head buried between her knees.

What could I say to comfort her? That she had paid for her crime? That psychiatry had made great strides in treating multiple personality disordert?

I had nothing to say. I sat in the nearby armchair, watching her every move. But she didn't stir. Every so often, her arms jerked under the strain, but she didn't loosen her grip. When her breathing became rhythmic, her arms dropped, and her head, wanting a more comfortable position, rested against the wood, I knew she had fallen asleep.

Still I kept vigil over that sorrowful child seeking refuge in her grandmother's wardrobe, over the woman that child had become, whose only consolation was to live the life of another woman who'd been dead 463 years.

TWENTY-TWO
Sorrow's Child

I kept watch over Licia until Carmelo walked into the attic. He didn't seem surprised at the scene. Perhaps this wasn't the first time he had found Licia asleep in her wardrobe. He came closer and whispered, "Rosa Catalino just called. Bernardina is supposed to take her the knapsack at three. Bernardina told Rosa she would. That's all."

I looked at my watch. It was half past one. I signaled for him to help me take Licia downstairs. She hardly stirred when he lifted her and carried her to her bedroom.

After I tucked Licia in bed, I left Carmelo at her side and went into my room to call Dora.

When I reached Dora, she informed me that two moving vans had been at the Legorretas' house the day before, according to one of their neighbors. Pretending to be a buyer looking over the grounds, Dora had also managed to check their mailbox. She had found a fat envelope from United Airlines.

"I have a friend who works for United in San Francisco," Dora said. "I asked her to find out if the Legorretas have reservations to travel to Mexico. They're booked on the red-eye to Mexico City on Sunday. If we're going to make a move, this is the time."

"To confront the Legorretas? And tell them what? We have no proof. No. Let's get Rosa Catalino to cooperate with us and give us more solid proof that Legorreta is involved in the illegal sale of drugs pre-Columbian artifacts and. If she does, we'll give her two hours to disappear before we get the police involved. That's the plan. Let's follow it."

A grunt at the other end of the line told me that, even if

unhappily, Dora agreed with me. "I'll see you at two-thirty."

Following my intuition, I called Mexicana Airlines next. Pretending to be Licia, I asked the reservations agent to confirm her departure for Mexico City. As I suspected, there had been a change, but the agent was reluctant to give me the new information. When his supervisor came on the line, I hung up.

I called Dora back and told her that we had to be ready to travel at a moment's notice. She was ready for any eventuality, she told me. But I realized I wasn't, so I called my mother and asked her to go to my house, pack some extra clothes for me, and leave the suitcase by the door. My mother had the good sense to know when to ask or not about my plans. Conscious that she would worry anyway, I reassured her I would let her know where I was going when the time came.

When I got back to Licia's bedroom, she was still asleep. Carmelo suggested that we ask Bernardina to watch over Licia for a while, but I told him it wasn't necessary for the time being. I was in great need of solitude and sleep myself. I welcomed the opportunity to sit and nap.

An hour later, the doorbell rang, but Licia still didn't move. I knew it was Dora at the door, but I waited until Bernardina came into the room to tell me about it. After asking her to stay with Licia, I picked up the knapsack, took it downstairs, and handed it to Dora.

"Later," Dora said and walked out.

I watched her go until I heard Licia's phone ring. A few seconds later, Carmelo announced from the kitchen that Michael Cisneros's secretary was on the phone. As he handed me the receiver, he told me he would be in the garage if I needed him.

After we exchanged greetings, Michael's secretary gave me the name Mario Quintero and two phone numbers where the man could be reached in Mexico. Mr. Quintero would be expecting my call. At Michael's request, she also had prepared a short profile of Mario Quintero. Since Licia didn't have a fax machine, she would be sending that to me shortly via messenger.

I had a sudden desire to call Justin in Los Angeles. I dialed his cell phone number, charging it to my phone card, but there was no answer. So I called his hotel. He wasn't in his room either. My voice quavered as I gave my name and number to the desk clerk. I shivered suddenly as if my face, neck, and arms had been exposed to extreme cold. Overwhelmed, I sat on a chair and covered my face with my hands until I could breathe with ease again.

When I finally took my hands away, I saw Licia standing in the doorway, looking intently at me. Bernardina peeked from behind her, then left. Soon I heard the sound of the vacuum cleaner somewhere on the second floor.

Licia's hair hung loose behind her back now; her eyes were still red and puffy, but she seemed in control. She got the tea kettle and filled it with water, then set it on the stove. She opened a canister and the aroma of cinnamon and orange filled the air. After putting a few scoops of the mixture into a teapot, she took out two mugs, spoons, and napkins and set them on the kitchen table. She sat down in front of me.

"It looks like we've both got troubles. Some tea will do us good," she said, flashing a smile. She seemed entirely different from the woman who, a few hours before, had curled up in her wardrobe.

"I'm sure it will. Thank you."

"Care to tell me about your problems?" she asked as she got up and poured boiling water into the teapot.

"Only if you tell me about yours first," I replied.

"I know you think I've lost my mind."

I only shook my head.

"I am not insane. I was not mad when I killed Peter. I knew what I was doing. He would have driven me to suicide or would have had me meet with an 'accident' of sorts," Licia said. "I truly believe that he had it all planned."

"Why didn't you just leave him—divorce him?"

"Did you have a good marriage?" she asked.

"Yes."

"Mine was a marriage made in Hell. But it wasn't so at the beginning. When I married Peter, I believed I was marrying a man who was loving, honest, someone incapable of deception. Only a few weeks after our wedding, he was transformed into the *other*, the man who slapped me every time I tried to talk about his business deals, or who shoved me away when I wanted sex or just to cuddle up with him in bed."

Licia seemed in control as she spoke, but her hand shook as she poured tea into the mugs. She was quiet for a while. She closed her eyes. I could see them, moving again rapidly under her eyelids. Afraid that another episode was coming, I touched her hand lightly. She opened her eyes. As if to allay my fear, she gave me a sad smile.

"Even to this day, I don't know if Peter loved me," she continued. "Perhaps he really did marry me for my money. All I know is that he began to drink to excess and destroy everything dear to me. The beatings began, and got worse. Secretly at first and then openly, my husband was calling his lovers, old and new. I'm not sure which I resented most, his real lovers or that other cruel mistress—alcohol," Licia said with a quavering voice. "I wanted so much to be loved by him. I did everything he wanted me to do."

She was quiet again, her gaze fixed on some distant point. For the first time I saw in her eyes Black Widow's unconsolable grief and sorrow—the pain I sensed in her when I first saw her on the Day of the Dead.

"Why did you stay with him?"

She bowed her head. "I'm not sure. I loved him very much. At first, I kept hoping that if I tried just a little harder, he would love me, that I would become indispensable in his life. A few months later, I just kept telling myself that I had to honor my marriage vows. Would you leave your husband if he developed cancer, even if the cancer was the result of a bad habit?"

I shook my head.

"Alcoholism is a disease," she continued. "But I was unable to cope with the abuse, so I began to see my confusion and depression as a weakness, a flaw in my character. I was the one at fault for not being able to give him strength. I couldn't make Peter happy because I wasn't good enough. I felt as though I had fallen into a vortex that grew stronger as I grew weaker. I wasn't eating properly. I would go days without enough sleep. Then one morning, as I got up, I fainted. I went to the doctor and found out that I was pregnant."

"Did *he* know you were pregnant?" I said as I sipped my tea, realizing that I was avoiding saying her husband's name.

"Yes. I thought it would make a difference and I told him I was expecting his baby. Peter seemed happy at first. He didn't touch a drop that evening. But the next day, he began to drink heavily, then spent most of the day out. When he came home that evening, he told me that it wasn't even his baby and accused me of trying to trap him. Trap him! We were married. So he ordered me to have an abortion. When I refused, he threw me on the floor and put his whole weight on my belly, pushing hard so I would miscarry. I thought he was going to kill me. But the doorbell rang at that moment. I didn't know it, but he had a woman, a blonde, waiting for him in the car. I guess she had gotten tired of waiting for him and had decided to find out what was taking him so long. Ironic, isn't it?" Licia said with a sad smile. "He went off with her and disappeared for three days. And . . . the rest is history."

For a while, I didn't know what to say. "Did you ever talk to his family about his abusive behavior?"

"No. Not really. His parents wouldn't have believed me anyway. I once confided in Isabela. She was the kindest of them, but she was also very afraid of her father's ill temper. Martín Lecuona was . . . *is* a tyrant. He squeezed the life out of his wife. Peter, more than anyone, was terrified of him."

I found ironic that Isabela Lecuona had married Legorreta, a man who seemed to be so like her father.

"Why are you telling me all this now?" I asked.

Licia hesitated, then said, "Because I need your help. I'm not sure how much you know about me."

"I know all that can be learned about you from others, people who care deeply about you."

"I see. Then you know what happened to my children," she said. When I nodded, she continued, "I have to see them and talk to them . . . Explain. I can't rest until I know they're safe and happy. Isabela loves them, I know that. But Legorreta . . . he's just Martín Lecuona's puppet. Together, they'll squeeze the life out of Inés and Martín, too. I have to stop them. You have to help me."

"For the time being, Licia, all I can do is try to keep you in one piece. Dora Saldaña and I believe that there is someone who can give us proof that Legorreta is involved in criminal activity. Right now, Dora is meeting with that person. But we can't do anything if we don't have your cooperation," I said. "Do you remember something, anything, about the person who stabbed you a week ago? Was he or she tall? Medium built? Fat? What was this person wearing?"

"I think it was a man because I could smell his cologne. He was taller than me, but he wasn't fat," Licia said, closing her eyes. Her breathing began to quicken. "It all happened so quickly. I saw the *conquistadores* coming at me, and that poor young woman running away from them. Suddenly, I was living a reality from long ago, something I had only seen in my mind. It terrified me. I tried to move out of the way, but I was paralyzed. Then, as the horsemen passed by me, I felt someone grab me. I tried to push him away, but he was stronger."

Licia was getting agitated, and I squeezed her arm lightly to reassure her.

"The man who attacked you, where did he come from?"

"He must have been hiding somewhere around there. I really don't know."

"Are you sure it wasn't one of the horsemen?" I asked.

She shook her head.

"Could he have been Juan Gabriel Legorreta?"

She opened her eyes, but she didn't look at me. "No. I know Legorreta's voice. I heard it so many times before. It wasn't him. This man had . . . I don't know how to explain it. He had a younger voice."

"So, this man said something to you. What did he say?" I asked eagerly.

"I'm not sure. I think he said, '*Déjalos en paz, puta asesina, o te mueres.'"*

"So he was threatening to kill you if you didn't leave the Legorretas alone. Did he say why?" I asked. Licia looked away and shrugged her shoulders. I didn't want her to shut herself in again. "Did this man have an accent?"

"What do you mean?" she said, raising her eyes.

"Was he a Mexican, or did he have a *gringo* accent in Spanish?"

"Not exactly, but he pronounced his esses like . . . Peter used to." She looked at me, astonished. I saw in her eyes the glimmer of a sudden realization.

"So he had a Spanish accent," I said.

She didn't answer. Visibly shaken, she got up. "I'm not feeling well," she said. "I'm going to go upstairs and lie down."

"Please wait. We're finally making progress."

"It's too late," she said.

She rushed out the kitchen door and up the stairs. Gradually my question was replaced by a more terrifying possibility. She knew who her assailant was. Worse yet, she was trying to protect him.

Who could be so important to her that she would risk her own life to protect?

The names of all the suspects flashed through my mind. I dismissed them all just as quickly. One name only, the name of the man I hadn't suspected at all, was left: Martín Legorreta.

TWENTY-THREE
The Lives of the Heart

Watching the second hand on the kitchen clock make its appointed rounds, I waited for the phone to ring.

While I waited, I reviewed everything I knew about Dr. Legorreta and young Martín. Painstakingly, I tried to convince myself that Martín could not possibly want his own mother dead. But did he even know that Licia was his mother? That she had killed his father? What argument had Professor Legorreta—and I was certain that he was behind it all—given his young son to make him a conspirator in such an enterprise?

I had no answers and I hated the inactivity. So I walked around the downstairs floor. I checked every window and door. Then, I went to the garage and talked with Carmelo, who was working on Licia's car. Finally, I went upstairs and found a book to read.

Back in the kitchen I read until the doorbell rang, announcing the arrival of the messenger from Michael's office. I signed for the envelope and went back into the kitchen. I tore the envelope open and began to read about Mario Quintero, our contact in Mexico.

Born in Tepoztlán, educated in Cuernavaca and Mexico City, Mario Quintero was about thirty-four years old, and the oldest son in a family of four children. His father and grandfather, owners of large land holdings and commercial farms, had both held prominent positions in Tepoztlán's city government. As a young man, Mario had been expected to continue the traditions started by his ancestors. But he decided instead to venture out of Mexico when he was twenty-one. He traveled to Chicago with his childhood friend, Manuel Lomas Covarrubias, who at present was a Lieutenant with the Grupo de Reacción—the Mexican equivalent to Special Forces—in the state of Morelos. After three years in Chicago, Manuel went back to Mexico and joined the Mexican army. But Mario stayed in Chicago another two years, until he received a letter from his mother notifying him of his grandfather's death. He went back to Tepoztlán, but his father, angry with him for having left, sent him away. He looked up his old friend, Manuel, and got a job with Special Forces.

In his handwriting, at the bottom of the page, Michael had added a message to me:

> *I met Mario and talked with him many times when I traveled to the Cuernavaca area as a member of several business delegations. I understand that at present he is not an active member of Grupo de Reacción, which pleases me. He is a good man, smart and capable, who got caught in a wave of 'criminal activity by other agents in the Grupo,' namely his friend, Lomas Covarrubias. Let me just say that you're in good hands. Good luck!*

I folded the note, slid it into my pants pocket, and went back to my silent vigil. At last the phone rang.

"No go," Dora said immediately. "Rosa doesn't have any evidence. She had it before, but she claims that Licia took the photos she had as proof. She never met Legorreta, but she suspected he was behind the smuggling of pre-Columbian jewels."

"How did she figure that out? How did she get hold of those photos?"

"Before she went to prison, she used to send small packages that came in with the drugs from the Oaxaca region to a P.O. Box in Livermore. She wanted to know who she was dealing with, so one day she staked out the post office. She took photos of a well-dressed man who picked up the mail and package. Rosa followed him to a house in the Livermore hills. She told me that at the time she didn't intend to blackmail him. When the narcs closed in on her, she sent her daughter to show Legorreta the photos. She kept the negatives at her house. Her house was burglarized and the negatives disappeared. Apparently, Licia has the only remaining copies of those photos. When Rosa went to jail and found out that Licia had killed Legorreta's brother-in-law, Rosa saw a way to get more information on him. She bribed a prison guard, who arranged for her to share the cell with Licia. But this woman—the same guard that told Licia about her babies—had a change of heart. She took the photos from Rosa and gave them to Licia. Rosa suspected as much, but, before she confronted Licia, she convinced her to hire Bernardina as her housekeeper. Her idea was to have the housekeeper get the photos back as soon as Licia was out of prison. But you know that without Rosa's testimony all of that amounts to a pile of manure in court."

"It isn't so hopeless," I said. "Rosa can make a deal with the police. Maybe, if Lester agrees, and I don't see why he wouldn't, he can represent her. Maybe the feds would then unseal the adoption files."

"That is, *if* we had her," Dora remarked.

"What do you mean?"

"She gave me the slip. She's gone," Dora said.

"How could that happen?" I asked, more astonished than annoyed.

"It happened," Dora replied abruptly. "I'm on my way to the Legorretas' house. Maybe they'll go back and pick up their mail. Or maybe I can convince their neighbor to tell me their whereabouts. I think Rosa's going to try to contact the professor again. I'll be in touch."

"Wait! Rosa isn't that foolish. Besides, if Legorreta gets wind that you're looking for him, he might leave the country ahead of schedule. Once he's in Mexico, the police here can't do anything. The children will be gone, too. We can't let that happen," I pleaded, but Dora had hung up.

As I turned the phone power off, I heard a creaking noise outside the door. I held my breath and listened again. Someone was going up or coming down the stairs. Cautiously, I stepped through the door and peeked. Bernardina was at the top of the stairs, turning onto the hall. I wondered if she had overheard my conversation with Dora. Since the situation with Rosa Catalino involved her, I could understand her curiosity. Afraid, nonetheless, that she would tell Licia about it, I decided to go upstairs and ask for her discretion.

I was about to knock on Licia's door, when I heard the women's voices inside. Instead, in the darkness, I walked through my room to the connecting door, which was ajar. Although the light was on in Licia's room, from my angle I couldn't see the two women, but I could hear them clearly.

"*Dijo que el profesor va a cambiar de planes y se va a llevar a sus hijos a México. Que nunca van a volver a los Estados Unidos,*" Bernardina said to Licia.

Licia was quiet until Bernardina left the room. Then she began to sob. I thought of going in and offering her words of comfort, but I knew words weren't enough to soothe her suffering. She was heartbroken, and I was impotent at the moment to do anything about it.

I refused to give into despair. I tried to block my own worries about Justin, but the greater my effort, the larger my sorrow and loneliness grew. I sat on my bed, in the darkened room, looking at the damned cell phone, like a shipwreck in the mist, listening for the splash of rescuing oars against the water, and hearing only the sound of immense space.

I closed my eyes and called on a vision, anything to fill the black void in my chest. But no vision about Licia came, only a dull pain on my left side just below my ribs, and the sensation of being suspended in mid-air. I opened my eyes. I thought once again that my visions had changed since my visit to Sister Rosa. Why, I wondered, as I moved towards the light switch in my room.

I didn't have a chance to turn on the light. I heard a scream, followed by a thump and the dull sound of something breaking downstairs. I got my gun from my handbag and grabbed the flashlight next to it, then rushed down the hall.

From the top of the stairs, I saw Bernardina standing with her back to the kitchen door, covering her mouth with her hands. Glass and ceramic shards lay strewn in front of her. The light in the kitchen was on, but she was blocking it.

I ran down the stairs and saw Carmelo wrestling with someone. The intruder was clad in black and wearing a death mask. By the way he moved and struggled, the intruder had to be a man. He had a knife. "The man in my dream. Please, God. Don't let him be Martín," I whispered.

"Stop or I'll shoot," I commanded, trying to aim my gun, but the two men were so close to each other that a clear shot was impossible. The opportunity came a few seconds later when Carmelo pushed the intruder away from him. As the man reeled back, the knife flew out of his hand, landing a few feet away. I released the safety and pointed the gun at him, but I kept my finger away from the trigger. The intruder, unarmed now, stood looking at me.

"Get the knife," I said to Carmelo. He didn't react. He seemed transfixed. Bernardina, too, stood with her mouth wide open, also staring at me.

I suddenly realized that all three were not looking at me but at someone behind me. I turned my head slightly and caught sight of Licia's white pants. Something pressed against my back, right below my right shoulder blade: Her knife. I cursed under my breath for not having taken it away from her earlier. It took all the willpower I had not to panic.

"Go back upstairs," I commanded Licia, in as firm a voice as I could muster. But she didn't move. "I am not your enemy," I said.

"Don't hurt him," Licia said.

"Put the knife down on the floor or I will," I told her. The pressure of the knifepoint on my back eased off. Out of the corner of my eye, I saw her lay the knife on the floor.

The intruder took a few steps towards us, getting closer to his own knife.

"Don't do it," I warned, still pointing the gun at him.

"Please, go. Now!" Licia pleaded. But he kept coming.

Before I had a chance to put my finger on the trigger, Licia grabbed my wrist. I pushed her away. She fell back, then tried to get up, but couldn't.

The intruder stretched his arms out in Licia's direction, then pulled them back. There was something familiar in his gesture, but I had no time to figure out its meaning, for he took a couple of steps back, then turned towards the front door.

"Grab him," I said to Carmelo.

Carmelo lunged towards the intruder, but missed him, crashing instead onto a small table. I saw him stumble as he got up, then fall on his knees. Bernardina screamed and took cover behind me. Licia grabbed my leg, and I had to struggle to free myself from her hold. In the confusion, the intruder darted out the front door.

"Call the police," I told Carmelo.

To Bernardina, I said, "Take care of Licia."

"No. No police," I heard Licia tell Carmelo as I ran out.

The man moved fast down. At the corner, I saw him stop. He stood briefly under the lamppost, then looked in all directions, as if waiting for someone.

When he saw me, he crossed the street. He started running up the stairs leading to the old hospital building. Since the building was no longer used for patient care, it was surely deserted. A good hiding place. I knew that we had now entered my vision. I put away my gun and ran after him.

When he saw the tall wrought iron fence blocking entrance to the old building, he stopped. He paced quickly from one side to the other, trying to find an avenue of escape.

I was halfway up the stairs when I saw him jump over a lower brick fence to a driveway on the other side. By the time I got to the spot, he was running alongside the building towards the outpatient clinic, but he didn't reach it. Just before he reached the parking lot next to the clinic, he turned. By the time, I got there, he had disappeared.

Panting, I reached the end of the path by the hospital laundry. The area outside the plant was well lit. I could see the tail end of a truck parked next to the building. I heard the sound of laughter and sought refuge next to the wall, then inched my way to the corner of the building, and peeked. Two men in white, laundry workers most likely, stood a few feet away, smoking and talking.

Mashed against the wall, I surveyed the area in all directions. In the parking lot beyond I saw two Highway Patrol black-and-whites parked side by side. As I took a second look at the walkway between two buildings behind me, I spotted the intruder. He was no longer running, but he walked at a good stride, headed in the direction we'd just come from.

I remembered that after he ran out of Licia's house, he had stopped at the corner as if he were waiting for someone to pick him up. It occurred to me that he might be looping back to that corner where someone waited for him. As I started to run, my cell phone rang. I slowed down, but I didn't stop.

"Dora," I said, and took a deep breath. "I can't talk to you. Get back to Licia's house now."

"Gloria?" I heard Justin say. "What's going on?"

Hearing his voice made my heart pick up a faster pace, robbing me of much needed breath. I stopped only long enough to say, "Sorry. I can't talk to you now. I'll call you." I pressed the power off.

Just my luck, I thought, as I slid down the ground covered with pine needles to get to the chicken-wire fence surrounding the area. I climbed over it and jumped onto the sidewalk. A short distance away, the intruder got into a Jaguar parked right at the corner. I ran across the street and towards the car as it backed up. It stopped under the street lamp for only an instant before it headed towards Fourteenth Avenue. I flashed my light on the driver and the passenger in the Jaguar.

"No, not him," I said aloud, as the car sped off. "How can God be so merciless?"

TWENTY-FOUR
Valley of The Fifth Sun

I started walking up the hill towards Licia's house. With every step, the answers that had eluded me when I saw Legorreta driving the getaway car became fearfully clear. But how could I tell Licia that her own son was trying to kill her?

Dora was getting out of her car when I reached the house.

"I phoned the house and Carmelo told me what happened. Did you catch him?" Dora asked.

"No," I said, then went on to explain what happened. I cursed softly.

"Know how you feel," she said and patted my shoulder.

We began to walk up the steps towards the front door, but we stopped briefly on the porch before entering.

"Did you find Rosa Catalino?" I asked.

"Nope. And the Legorretas are gone. Well, I mean, we know where two of them were, but Isabela and Inés have flown the coop, too," she said. "I have the feeling that they'll be heading to SFO soon. I took the liberty of finding out about the flights to Mexico tonight. There are two possibilities: a United flight that leaves at nine forty-five, and another at eleven. We could try to stop them at the gate. What do you think?"

Before I could tell Dora that I had no idea what our next move was, the door opened.

"She's gone. *La señora* Licia is gone. I'm sorry," Carmelo said in an agrieved tone.

"Gone? Gone where?" Dora asked. "How could you let that happen?"

"It's okay. It's not your fault. It's no one's fault," I reassured Carmelo and headed up the stairs to the attic. The secret compartment in the wardrobe was empty.

I went back downstairs. "Do you know if Licia has any contacts or friends in Mexico City?"

"I don't know. But like you told me, I took her upstairs. She was very upset. So I stayed by the door. I heard her talking to someone. She said she was coming to see whoever was at the other end tomorrow morning. I know I shouldn't have done it, spy on her, but I opened the door quietly and saw her writing something on a pad next to the phone. Then I went downstairs to tell Bernardina to make dinner and went to clean up the garage. *La señora* Licia must have left at that time. Bernardina says that she didn't hear her go either."

Dora and I looked at each other. I headed towards the stairs.

"You did good," Dora said to Carmelo and patted his hand, then followed me up to Licia's bedroom.

We found the pad, still on Licia's night table. Dora found a pencil and began to rub the paper lightly with the side of the point. "Not clear. Wait," she said. "There. Looks like some numbers 504-07 something. It says, 'Cross Plaza,' then something . . . then 'Conchita,' then 'Coyoa' . . . I can't make out the rest." She stared at the paper for a moment then added, "Coyoacán. That's it. She's meeting someone in Coyoacán. That's in Mexico City, isn't it?"

I answered her with a nod. "That's where we're going. Get on the phone and see if you can get us on one of those flights tonight. Then go home and get your stuff. Let me know which flight before you leave. I'll call Michael Cisneros and Quintero, our contact in Mexico City." I looked at my watch and was surprised to see it was seven o'clock already. "Let's meet here in about an hour, eight or so. I'll ask Carmelo to drive us to the airport."

"Should I pack my . . . you know," she asked.

"No. No weapons. It's all arranged with Quintero. Let's get to it," I said.

"Yes, ma'am," Dora said and smiled. I left her upstairs calling the airlines and went downstairs to talk to Carmelo. Then I called Michael Cisneros and informed him about Licia's disappearance and our plans. Dora came into the kitchen with the flight information.

I looked at the slip of paper she handed me with our flight confirmation number. "First class?"

"The only way to fly," she said. "In fact, the only seats we could get. Any problem?"

"No problem," I answered, hoping that Michael would not object. "Did you tell Lester about it?"

"Yes. I just called him," she replied, then headed out.

From the kitchen phone, I called Quintero in Mexico. Luckily, he was at home. Although our conversation began in Spanish, we soon switched to English, which he spoke fairly well. I gave him our flight information, then asked him if he was familiar with the Coyoacán area and with a Plaza-Something-Conchita there or anywhere else in the city.

"La Plaza de la Conchita," he said. "It's in Coyoacán. There is a small chapel there, at the plaza. It's not used often, the church. Occasional weddings, baptisms, maybe. It's near the old Hacienda de Cortés."

"Are you familiar with the history of that particular area?" I asked.

"It depends. Coyoacán is a very old place. What period are you talking about?"

"The Conquest," I replied, "Malinche and Cortés."

He thought for a moment. Then, in an apologetic tone, he said, "Not as familiar as I should be. But if it's important for your business here, I'll find out. I have a friend, a historian. He can answer all your questions."

"Would you mind asking your friend the historian where Malinche's house in Coyoacán was? Right away? It's very important."

"Sure," he answered. "Michael asked me to find out about the Lecuona family. They don't live in Cuernavaca any more. They have a big ranch in the mountains, just outside Tepoztlán. It is not far from Cuernavaca. If you're planning to go there, bring a pair of good hiking shoes. But I have to tell you, they are well-con-

nected. Friends of the governor and others even higher up."
Quintero paused briefly, perhaps waiting for my reaction. Then he
said, "Ah, yes, about *la herramienta.* You can select the weapon
you like when you get here."

I thanked him, gave him a detailed description of Dora and
myself, and hung up.

I went to my house to repack my bag and get my affairs in
order. Then I took a quick trip to the office and taped a memo on
Justin's personal voice mail. I brought him up to date and gave
him Quintero's numbers in Mexico City and Tepoztlán. I told him
to also check with my mother, as I would try to call her as often
as possible. I called my daughter Tania and finally my mother.
Even if my destination was only forty miles away, every time I
traveled, my mother gave me her blessing. But this time, her voice
broke slightly as she did. I reassured her I had every intention of
coming back alive.

"I love you, Mom," I said and I was surprised at how much
my voice sounded like that of a little girl.

"I love you, too, *m'ija*, very much. I'll ask Saint Christopher
to watch over you."

I didn't have the heart to remind my mother that Saint
Christopher was among those stripped of their saintly power by
the Pope. In Heaven, as on earth, no one was indispensable, I
thought. But if things in Heaven worked as on earth, he probably
had been replaced, and his substitute might hear my mother's
prayer. I had the feeling I was going to need each one of those
prayers.

Carmelo came in with a very small, worn-out leather sack. "I
want you to have this. It's kept me safe many times. It'll protect
you, too." I opened it and saw the green stone in it.

I put the tiny sack in my shirt pocket and held his hand in
mine for a few seconds to thank him for his thoughtfulness.

"We'll be at any of these numbers," I said as I scribbled Mario
Quintero's numbers in Mexico and handed him the slip of paper.
"If you happen to hear from Licia, please call me."

Bernardina came out as Dora and I were ready to leave.

"Don't worry. *La señora* Licia is okay," she tried to reassure me, but her hand was shaking as she handed me my handbag.

An hour later, Dora and I arrived at the San Francisco airport. Since we were traveling first class, checking in went smoothly. But instead of going to the first-class passenger lounge, we strolled around the terminal, hoping to catch a glimpse of Licia. She was nowhere to be seen.

As we were boarding, I took one last look at the other gates. I nudged Dora's arm and said, "The Legorretas."

"They're coming this way," Dora said.

We both watched them make their way to the end of the line at our ticket counter.

"This is our lucky night. Shall we go over there and introduce ourselves?" she asked and laughed. "Just kidding," she reassured me when she saw me frown. "But seriously, once they're in Mexico, no one can touch them. So what do we do?"

"By the time the Oakland Police notifies the South San Francisco Police, they'll be gone. And we'll be tied up here while they—and Licia—are in Mexico. Our job is to find Licia and to see that no harm comes to her," I said. But, like Dora, I would have loved nothing more than to put a little fear in Legorreta's heart. "Let's see what happens when we get to Mexico City," I told Dora, as we walked down the jetway.

"If you don't mind, I'll take the aisle seat," Dora said and I agreed.

Ten minutes later, the Legorretas boarded. Inés and Martín walked ahead of Legorreta while Isabela trailed behind him. Inés either had a cold or had been crying, for her eyes and nose were red. Martín was pale and sullen, moving slowly down the aisle, despite his father's nagging, or perhaps because of it. Every so often, he looked briefly over his shoulder as if expecting someone.

Since I had the window seat, I pretended to look out to avoid detection. When I thought it was safe, I turned around and threw a quick glance over my head rest. Legorreta seemed quite mortified by a first-class passenger who was retrieving his tote case from the overhead compartment. He took a step back and so did

Isabela behind him, brushing Dora's arm. She looked at Dora and offered an apology. Then, she glanced at me. Our eyes met for an instant and I saw a glimmer of recognition, then fear in hers. Perhaps she saw the same fear in mine, for, unexpectedly, she smiled. Not knowing what else to do, I smiled and greeted her with a nod of my head, hoping that her smile was one of complicity, not deceit.

The rest of the flight was uneventful. I was too restless to attempt sleep, but I managed to do some reading for a while. I left the surveillance of the Legorretas to Dora, who made a few trips to the rear restroom so she could check on them. Concerned about Dora's "discomfort," an elderly woman sitting across the aisle offered her some anti-diarrhea medicine. Graciously, Dora declined. She and the woman chatted for a while. But when the flight attendant suggested that Dora use the more convenient restroom next to the cockpit, she said, "So what if I like slumming?" From that point on, the flight attendants were polite but not friendly.

I looked out the window as the plane began to turn towards the airport. It was only four-thirty in the morning in Mexico, but the city was already awake. Perhaps it had never really slept, I thought.

Bernal Díaz, in his *Chronicle of the Conquest of the New Spain*, had marveled at the beauty and organization of the great Tenochtitlan, unparalleled by any city of the old world in the sixteenth century. I wondered what he would say now, looking at the smoggy, noisy, throbbing metropolis the ancient city had become. The old Aztec capital sprawled now from end to end of a valley seventy-five-hundred feet above sea level and crawled up the surrounding mountains. As in ancient times, it was still guarded by the restless, enigmatic Popocatepetl and the sleeping Ixtacihuatl, the snow-capped legendary volcanoes, now eternally hidden behind the veil of smog.

As the plane shook and rattled under the strain of the landing, I tried not to think of the old Aztec prediction that this valley and everyone in it would succumb on the day Four-Earthquake of the

Fifth Sun. Anthropologists hadn't been able to determine yet when that day would come. Remembering the seismic activity in the Valley of the Fifth Sun in the last few years, I prayed that this day struggling with the toxic haze to dawn over the mountains wasn't Four-Earthquake.

TWENTY-FIVE
Reprieve from Fear

We had lost track of the Legorretas when we went through Immigration. But I caught sight of them behind us in the baggage area. Due to the large number of air travelers, Mexican airport authorities had instituted a lottery system for the customs area. Before entering that area, travelers were asked to push a button on a panel that had a green and a red light. At the check point, I got the green light, but Dora had to have her bags inspected.

As I waited for her, the Legorretas came up to the check point. Even before Isabela stretched her hand out to push the button, a man clad in a dark jacket and pants and sunglasses approached them. He talked to the guard at the gate and showed him some documents. The guard looked at the papers, then signaled for the whole group to move out.

Outside the gate area, the man with the dark glasses called a skycap to help them with their bags. He spotted another man nearby and went to talk to him. The second man wore a hat and boots. They had a brief exchange and shook hands. The man in dark joined the Legorretas again, but the other remained in the area. The Legorretas and their escorts disappeared into the crowd at the International Arrivals area, as Dora handed her authorized customs form to the gate officer.

Before I had a chance to tell Dora what I'd seen, the man with the hat began to walk towards us. My paranoia hit a critical level, and it took every ounce of courage I had in me to stand still. Unaware, Dora kept saying, "Where is he?"

"I am Mario Quintero," the man said. "You must be Gloria Damasco and Dora Saldaña."

Before I had a chance to say anything, Dora asked, "May we

see your ID?"

The man laughed, but took out his wallet. He showed Dora his driver's license and Mexican draft card. She looked at them. Satisfied, she said, "I'm Dora. It's a pleasure to meet you, Mario Quintero."

"Likewise," I said. "Could you please wait for me?"

"Where are you going?" Dora said. "The restroom is over there," she said, pointing in the direction opposite the one I was heading towards.

"I'll be right back," I said and ran out the nearest exit door, then walked along the curb. I spotted the skycap putting the last of the Legorretas' bags into a dark olive van. All sorts of antennae protruded from its roof, making it look like a huge green cockroach. I watched the van go, feeling like the chief of police in the movie *Jaws* when he sees the monstrous great white shark and says to the boat captain, "We're going to need a bigger boat."

"What was that all about?" Dora asked when I rejoined them.

I signaled for her to wait. Instead I addressed our host, "Tell me. Who was that man in the dark glasses you were talking to outside the gate?"

"Lomas Covarrubias. He's with the Grupo de Reacción. He works for the governor of Morelos. We used to work together," he answered. His gaze was intense, but his manner was straightforward. In his voice, I detected no desire to deceive us. What I did sense was a great deal of conflict in this man, who was perhaps no older than thirty-five.

"Did you know that the people he was escorting are the Legorretas and that they're related to the Lecuonas?"

"No, I didn't know. But that explains why you were watching their every move," he said and gave me an ample smile.

I wasn't surprised he had recognized me, since I had given him a very good description of both Dora and myself. Also, since he had been an agent in the special forces guarding the governor, his powers of observation were probably above the ordinary. I was intrigued and wanted to ask him why he had quit the special forces, but it was neither the time nor the place.

Dora, impressed with his surveillance skills, paid him a compliment. He shrugged his shoulders slightly, a gesture I interpreted as self-assurance. "If we're going to make it to Coyoacán before nine o'clock, we'd better go. We can stop and eat something if you'd like," he said. He offered to help us with our suitcases, but Dora and I turned him down. Our self-sufficient attitude didn't seem to bother him.

We reached his car, an old Thunderbird, which in the States was beginning to be considered a collector's car. He unlocked the car doors, then put our bags in the trunk. I slid into the back seat and Dora got in the passenger side. She picked up a large empty bottle of Coca-Cola, then put it down again, as she said, "You don't see this in the States anymore."

"Please, forgive the mess. This is my younger brother's car. I own a four-wheel-drive Cherokee. But it's an odd number day and mine couldn't circulate today," he told us. He explained that to minimize automobile toxic emissions, the government had set up a license plate system for motorists to correspond with odd-even-numbered days. The system applied to anyone driving in Mexico City, regardless of place of origin. Since his license plate ended in an even number and that day was odd-numbered, his car could not circulate in Mexico City.

Without taking his eyes off the road except for brief glances at the rearview and side mirrors, Mario tried to answer Dora's questions about the different places and monuments along the way. Then, their conversation took a different turn as they began to talk about the Chicano political movement in the States. I stayed out of the conversation but listened attentively to their discussion about the differences between Mexican and Chicano cultures, and the desire on the part of Chicanos to be acknowledged by Mexicans.

"But why is it so important for Chicanos to be accepted by us, by Mexican people?" Mario asked with genuine interest.

"Let me put it to you this way," Dora began. "We Chicanos are like the abandoned children of divorced cultures. We are forever longing to be loved by an absent neglectful parent—

Mexico—and also to be truly accepted by the other parent—the United States. We want bicultural harmony. We need it to survive. We struggle to achieve it. That struggle keeps us alive. Does that make sense to you?"

Mario laughed wholeheartedly. "Only a smart woman would come up with such a good analogy," he commented, looking at me in the rearview mirror.

A few sun rays were finally breaking through the layers of smog when we arrived in Coyoacán. I noticed the difference in architecture as soon as we arrived in it. It exuded a feeling of quiet fortitude and pride, the same feeling I'd experienced in the smaller colonial cities of Guanajuato and San Miguel de Allende, where Darío and I had spent our happiest time in Mexico ten years before.

It was only seven o'clock in the morning, but the main Plaza in Coyoacán was already bursting with activity. Local artisans were busy setting up their arts and crafts booths for the Sunday open market—the *tianguis*. Less fortunate vendors, who couldn't afford the trappings, placed their merchandise on blankets on the stone ground. Others peddled their wares on foot to early tourists not eager yet to start their shopping sprees on empty stomachs.

Not far from where we stood, a barefoot, giggly three-year-old girl watched a puppeteer make his puppet *charro* dance to the *Son de La Negra,* sung by an older boy who accompanied himself by stroking the ridges on an empty plastic water bottle with a small comb.

A group of young girls with all sorts of necklaces hanging from their arms spotted us immediately. Like birds spreading their jeweled wings, they ran towards us, scaring away the pigeons that searched for crumbs in the crevices and cracks among the cold stones.

"*Cómprame a mí,*" they each shouted, choosing a necklace and waving it in front of us as far as their short arms could reach. Dora gave into a few demands right away and ended up with four necklaces, all chosen by Mario at her request. Thinking they would make pretty gifts for my mother, my daughter, and Nina, I also

acknowledgements

Many, many thanks to Venetia Gosling, a *brilliant* editor. She leads a fantastic team at Macmillan; without Talya Baker and Fliss Stevens, the all-important final furlong would have taken forever. Thanks also to Rachel Vale for designing a very striking cover. Lots of people are involved in publishing a book, and at this stage (more than three months before publication) I'm not sure who will yet come to the fore, so apologies if I owe you and don't yet know it.

The manuscript would be in a drawer at home were it not for Gillie Russell at Aitken Alexander. She's great. Gillie made crucial suggestions when the first draft appeared and held my hand throughout the publishing process.

TAS and AMC were helpful young critics—many thanks. Thanks also to "Reg" Sansom, Charles Phillips and Susan Richards: you let me know that *Thirteen* worked as a story.

I was inspired to keep going by she who is always on my mind. Thanks to you. I'll write the book about aliens sometime.

The book is dedicated to the essential pair of TWSG and AW. They didn't laugh when I said that I would write a book in the summer holidays and were of huge significance throughout.

bought three.

The pealing of bells alerted the girls to parishioners arriving to hear Sunday Mass. Seeking prospective buyers, they ran towards the opposite end of the plaza where the cathedral was. We walked into one of the small restaurants off the plaza and ordered coffee, hot chocolate, and *pan dulce*. The restaurant had just opened and the only waitress on duty took our order and disappeared into the kitchen.

"You speak English well. Where did you learn it?" Dora asked Mario.

"From many North American tourists who've been coming to Tepoztlán every summer. I also lived in Chicago almost five years, the hardest years of my life," he said.

"How did you end up in Chicago?" I asked.

"Manuel Lomas Covarrubias, the man at the airport, and I decided to run away together. We were twenty-one years old, from Tepoztlán, and tired of waiting for things to change. Tepoztecos, we are like you Chicanos, children of opposing cultures, always struggling to keep our cultural equilibrium. Most indigenous communities like Tepoztlán go through the same struggle. But I didn't understand that until I lived in Chicago," he said. "Those years in the U.S. changed us, Manuel and me. We swore never to feel so helpless, so powerless again."

"Is that why you both joined the special forces?" Dora asked.

"Yes. Not a very smart move. Let's just say that after a couple of years I wasn't willing to pay the price for the use of that power. Special forces are a sort of elite, serving at the command and whim of people who listen little to their consciences. I lost the respect of my father and everyone in the town. But I didn't know how to get out."

"Does that mean you're still a member?" Dora asked.

"No. As my mother says, Providence was watching over me. But everything comes with a price tag, doesn't it? My father died, suddenly, of a heart attack. My mother became very ill. She and my sisters were left without anyone to look after them. I was the oldest and my brother too young to take care of things at home.

I'm sure you'll find this ironic, but there is a code of honor, especially among those in special forces. Family is very important," he explained.

"Not unusual at all. The *mafiosi* believe that, too. So do the homeboys in Oakland," Dora remarked.

Mario laughed, then continued, "I went to Manuel who, in a few years, had moved up the ranks to lieutenant. I explained about my dilemma. He talked to our superiors and arranged that I be allowed to return to Tepoztlán until I could get my family affairs in order. That was six months ago."

"Are you planning to go back?" I asked.

"No. I'm not. Power and freedom are great responsilibities. Most people, especially those in the special forces, don't know how not to abuse them. But I don't know yet how I'm going to get out of it."

We finished our meal in silence. I tried to enjoy the moment and not to think of Justin and the prospect of my life without him. Supressing my feelings for him made me feel more anxious, so I finally let my memory of him surface. That and the three cups of hot chocolate I drank warmed my heart again.

Dora paid for our meal with the understanding that the next one would go on my expense account.

Although it was only eight, I asked Mario to take us to the Plaza de la Conchita.

"You were right, Gloria," he said as he drove around. "That's the Casa de La Malinche right across from the Plaza de La Conchita there." He pointed at a corner house painted a dark orange, then at the plaza and the small church at the opposite end. The front door of the house faced the plaza. It was a huge carriage door with a smaller door imbedded in it to let people in without having to open the larger one. I imagined it opened onto a courtyard, probably used as a garage now.

"My friend, the historian, told me that Hernán Cortés had that chapel built so that Doña Marina, La Malinche, could go to Mass. Apparently, she became quite a devout Catholic and went to church every day."

Mario parked the car. Before getting out, I took out the newspaper clipping with the then-and-now photos of Licia and showed it to Mario. "She always dresses in white," I told him as we got out.

Mario and Dora stayed by the car. I walked around the plaza, always keeping an eye on Malinche's house. I felt cold and tired and I was beginning to feel lightheaded, partly because of the lack of sleep and partly, I assumed, due to the high altitude. So I found a sunny spot from which I could continue my surveillance of the house and keep Mario and Dora in sight. They talked all the while as if they had known each other for a long time. I caught myself wondering if they had been lovers in a previous life. That thought led to others, and, little by little, my mind began to roam over a vast continent of memories of Darío's and my life together, then over the small territory of my relationship with Justin. I decided that I no longer subscribed to Mami Julia's notion that it was more important in life to love than to be loved.

My reverie was interrupted when I noticed a woman coming out of Malinche's house through the small door. She was carrying a broom, dustpan, and pail. She began to sweep the sidewalk all around the house, leaving the pail by the open door. Wanting to take a look at the inside of the house, I walked across the plaza and the street. The woman was cleaning the sidewalk around the corner from the house and didn't notice me.

I stepped onto the courtyard. Under arches, a long corridor provided shelter from rain or sun to the rooms that opened onto it. Except for the door to the kitchen, the other doors were now closed. I was about to walk over to the kitchen door when I heard the noise of metal crashing on stone behind me. I turned around to face the fear-filled eyes of the woman who'd been sweeping the street. Upon seeing me, she had dropped the pail, spilling its contents on the courtyard floor.

Brandishing the broom like a lance and trying to sound firm, she questioned my business there. "*¿Qué quiere aquí?*"

"*Busco a la señora Licia,*" I said, taking a chance.

She told me that such a woman didn't live in the house. I tried to explain that she didn't live there but was expected.

The woman thought for a moment, then said, "*Los señores andan de viaje.*"

I was a bit baffled at her explanation that the people who lived there were traveling. I remembered that Bernardina had mentioned that she had an uncle who lived in Coyoacán.

"*¿Conoce usted a Bernardina Lorenzo? Ella vive en California,*" I asked, hoping that she knew Bernardina.

She thought for a moment then asked, "*¿La sobrina de don Remigio?*"

"*Sí,*" I answered. Assuming that Don Remigio was Bernardina's uncle and possibly Licia's contact, I asked the woman if she knew where I could find Don Remigio.

She explained that she knew Don Remigio, but that he didn't live in the Malinche house. She then walked out the gate. I followed her out. Pointing at a house down the block, she said, "*Vive ahí, en esa casa.*"

From what she said next, I gathered that Don Remigio didn't have a phone and he got some calls at the house in exchange for odd jobs. A woman had called him early, from the airport. Don Remigio's niece in California worked for the woman he was meeting at the airport. He had packed a bag and had told her that he would be gone for a few days. She was supposed to look after his parrots.

I thanked her and apologized for my intrusion. I picked up the pail, handed it to her, and rushed out to give Dora and Mario the news. The car was still there, but Dora and Mario were nowhere near it. I looked around and finally spotted them searching the plaza for me. I called their names aloud and they came running. I told them about my conversation with the woman at the house. Then, we quickly made our way to the car.

"We have to find a phone to call Carmelo," I said. "I have a strong feeling that Bernardina is Don Remigio's niece. It's the only possible explanation. Otherwise, how in heaven would Licia know anyone in Mexico City?"

Agreeing with me, Mario drove us back to the main plaza to

find a long-distance phone.

When Carmelo answered the phone, he immediately said, "I just called Mr. Quintero's house, looking for you."

"Did you hear from Licia?" I asked.

"No. I wanted to tell you what Bernardina said to me, that no harm was going to come to Licia because her Uncle Remigio—Bernardina's uncle—was looking after her. He's taking her to Cuernavaca."

"Did she tell you where in Cuernavaca? What hotel?"

"No. I really think she doesn't know."

"I'm not too sure of that," I said. "She's been keeping a lot of things from us. Keep pressing her. Maybe she'll tell you."

He reassured me he would call me if he was able to find out where Licia was staying.

Agreeing that Licia would try to find her way to the Lecuona's ranch, Mario, Dora and I decided to go directly to Tepoztlán.

Despite my anxiety, or perhaps because of the adrenaline pumping steadily since we left Coyoacán, I felt invigorated. Soon, Mario's car was climbing up the mountains on a four-lane modern highway that offered impressive views of the Valley of Mexico behind us and the eight-shaped Valley of Cuaunahuac—the valley of my vision at Rosa Catalino's house. The city of Cuernavaca leisurely spread over its northern half. Small towns lay basking in the sunlight in its southern half. The Sierra de Tepoztlán rose in the east.

As we turned onto a two-lane road, Mario said, pointing at a place somewhere up one of the mountains, "That's where I live. A magic and sacred place."

TWENTY-SIX
The Jade-eyed God's Domain

The air felt cooler but the sun was shining bright as we entered the high valley of Tepoztlán. One mountain had the shape of a modern-day observatory, another the shape of a gigantic man. Quarries, like medieval castles or skyscrapers, rose all around us, amidst exuberant vegetation. Every so often, I saw the mouths of caverns, partly hidden by forests of holm oak, spruce, torch-pine and madrone. During the Revolution of 1910, protected and aided by the Tepoztecos, Emiliano Zapata had hidden from the government army in one of those caverns, Mario said. He also told us that Cortés, believing that Moctezuma's treasure was buried there, had ordered his soldiers to search those caverns.

Dora and I were in awe of such majestic beauty. And, for a while, we forgot about Licia and the Lecuonas, and the danger that awaited us.

The road we traversed came to an oak tree and wound around it. It was an old but ordinary tree, of no special significance or beauty. I didn't have to ask why the road had been laid around it, for the oak itself was testimony of the Tepoztecos' respect for nature and their desire to co-exist with it.

At midmorning on Sunday, Tepoztlán was far from being a sleepy town, lost in the Ajusco Range. I felt its vitality and vibrancy the minute we arrived.

Mario drove around the marketplace to one of the streets fanning from the main plaza, and parked. He had to talk to a friend, an archeologist and violin maker, who could help us should we need it. It was better if we didn't meet him for the time being. He suggested that we go to the *tianguis* and meet him back at the car in twenty minutes.

With its colorful displays of silver crafts, masks, pottery, decorative and edible flowers, and fruit, Tepoztlán's Sunday market was a feast for the eyes, and a sonata of birdsong, church bell's laughter, and chatter.

My spirit felt lighter than it had in many days. I suspected that the tourists from Mexico City, Cuernavaca, and the United States came to Tepoztlán to soak up some of its invigorating energy and to rediscover the magic in their lives. Perhaps this was the reason that Mario had referred to this valley as a magic and sacred place.

Dora and I were about to walk into a clothing store when we caught sight of Isabela, Inés and Martín Legorreta at a fruit stand. I looked around, trying to spot Professor Legorreta, but he was nowhere in sight. Isabela gave her children some money and they took off. With a smile on her face, she watched them go for a while.

"Licia must be around," Dora said, echoing my thought. "Should we follow the children?" she asked.

"Maybe it's better if you do. Licia won't be expecting you. If she sees me, she won't come out in the open. Don't attempt anything on your own. Let's meet back at the car as planned."

"What are you going to do?" she asked, already a few feet away from me.

"I'm going to have a talk with Isabela."

I crossed the street. Isabela looked in my direction. She put the fruit in the basket she was carrying, but she continued talking to the woman at the fruit stand. When I was close enough, she suddenly turned around and asked, "What are you doing here? You were at my house, pretending to be a lawyer. I saw you on the plane, too. Who are you really? What do you want?"

"I was hired to protect Licia, your sister-in-law. Someone has been trying to kill her," I said and waited for her reaction, but she kept quiet. "Look, I think I know who's trying to kill her. Don't you think it's time that you do something about it? If you don't, Martín will lose his eternal soul and you will lose him forever."

I was surprised at my own words. I had intended to say that he would lose his life.

"He's still a child," she said.

"He won't be a child anymore if he becomes . . . if he succeeds in this tragic enterprise," I said.

Isabela's eyes began to move rapidly from side to side. The struggle between her conscience and her love for her son was written all over her pained face.

My heart felt for her, but I pressed on. "This is not your son's debt to anyone, most of all to your husband or to your brother Peter," I said.

"You don't understand," Isabela replied, wiping a tear from her eyes. "I'm the one who's responsible for this mess. I wanted children, but Juan didn't. When we found out that Licia was pregnant, we had no idea she was going to have twins. I went to my father and pleaded with him to get me the child. My father agreed and Juan, who would do anything my father asked, agreed, too. You see, Juan came from a very poor Mexican-American family. My father helped him to get an education. He is extremely loyal to my father. He'll do anything to please my father. Just like Martín will do anything to please Juan." Isabela paused. "Juan doesn't know any other way to be a man but to be like my father. Since my son was very young, Juan dealt with Martín the way my father dealt with him—punishing him at the first sign of weakness." She paused again, then said, "It's my fault. I taught my children to obey their father without question, so he would love them. I insisted on it. Juan is not responsible; I am. I was the one who wanted children."

"Regardless of who wanted, or not, the children, it's wicked for Juan to involve your children—your son, in particular—in his criminal activities," I tried to reassure her.

She gave me a sad smile, but said nothing.

"Do your children know that Licia is their mother?"

"I . . . I don't think so," she answered after a while.

"But you're not sure." I paused to give myself time to gather my thoughts, then said, "I don't know about Inés, but I have the feeling that Martín knows Licia is his mother. Not only that, I also suspect that your husband told him that Licia killed Peter. How else would Juan convince Martín to go along with his plan on the Day of the Dead in San Francisco? Am I wrong?"

Isabela's face turned red, and the hollow under her chin pulsated visibly.

"I was there. I saw it all. That's how I got involved in this case. It was Martín who stabbed Licia that night. Martín was the acrobat I saw running away from the scene, wasn't he?"

Isabela gasped for breath, then began to sob. I put my arm around her shoulder.

"It wasn't meant to happen like that. It was an accident. You see, Juan just wanted to scare Licia away. He told Martín that Licia had forged some documents that incriminated him and my father as taking part in some illegal business, that he and my father would end up in prison and we would be left homeless. That's what Juan told me he'd said to Martín. I . . ."

"You don't really believe that's all he said, do you?"

Isabela kept quiet, but she didn't make a move to leave.

"Were you and your husband dressed as *conquistadores* that night? Who was the woman in black?"

"*Conquistadores?* I don't know who they were," she answered.

"Are you sure?"

"Of course I'm sure."

My heart skipped a beat. The suspicion that I had experienced a regression to a past life, or, worse yet, a hallucination, left me breathless for a few seconds.

Looking at my bewildered expression, Isabela took a step back. Her mouth opened and closed again.

"It's all right," I said, quickly recovering from my surprise. "I intend no harm to you or your children. On the contrary. I think you know I'm here only to avert a tragedy. But tell me something, how did you know that Licia was going to be at the Day of the Dead procession?"

Isabela hesitated. "Licia herself called us. We were supposed to meet her at Balmy Street after the procession. If we didn't show up, she threatened to turn in the evidence she had to the police, not only about the illegal adoption but of Juan's business deals in

Mexico. Juan panicked. I begged him then to let the children and me come to Mexico and stay here until it all blew over. Unfortunately, he called my father for advice, and my father told him to 'deal with the problem' or face the consequences," she said bitterly. "So he came up with that ill-fated plan on the Day of the Dead. But he didn't count on Martín telling Inés about it. The night of the procession, Inés ran away from us and tried to warn Licia. My poor, foolish daughter . . . We had to go after her. If you were there, you know what happened," she added.

"And he sent Martín to Licia's house last night to do his dirty work again," I said. "Quite a man, your husband."

She lowered her head. When she looked at me again, she said, "We're here, in Mexico. Everything will be okay now. I know it."

"No. I'm afraid not," I said. "Why do you think I'm here too? Licia is here, in Cuernavaca."

Isabela dropped her arms and let the basket go. Oranges and apples spilled to the floor like marbles from a child's hand. People around us rushed to help me gather the scattered fruit.

I put the fruit back in the basket as it was handed to me, then I gave it to Isabela. She took it with an automatic gesture. Her face was pale, her eyes and mouth wide open. She took a step but stumbled back. I put my arms around her to keep her steady. The woman at the fruit stand rushed out with a stool. I made Isabela sit on it. The fruit vendor found a folded newspaper and began to fan Isabela's face. I thanked her.

When Isabela regained her composure, I said, "Look. Licia wants to see Inés and Martín. That may be enough for her for the time being."

"I can't let her see them," Isabela said. She stood up. "I'm not ready to let her have my children."

"She'll be killed unless you intervene. Are you ready to live with that?" I asked.

"No one is going to kill her. We are in Mexico now. She can't do anything about anything."

I scribbled Mario's phone number on the back of my business card and handed it to her. "Call me if you change your mind."

She didn't look at my card but put it in her purse. I watched her go and prayed that, like before, she would not mention our meeting to her husband. I turned around and headed towards the car, trying to decide if my seeing the conquistadors after the procession was a regression or a hallucination.

Not wanting to pursue questions that defied logical explanation, I stepped up my pace.

TWENTY-SEVEN
Supplicants at La Santísima

When I got back to the car, Mario was already waiting. I told him about my conversation with Isabela Legorreta. Then, he told me that his friend, the archeologist, was ready to assist us in any way possible. In exchange, he wanted any pre-Columbian pieces we came across.

Dora returned ten minutes later. "Those kids looked at everything, and bought just as much," she said and leaned against the hood of the car, fanning her face with her hand.

"Where are they now?" I asked.

"Looking at tapes," she answered, then added, "No sign of Licia."

On our way to Mario's house, I brought Dora up to date.

Fifteen minutes later we arrived at Mario's farm, not too far from a mountain called the Tlacatepetl or Man's Mountain. Rows of tilled soil extended, like a peacock's fantail, from a large grove of trees in the center to the foot of the mountain. As we approached, a series of buildings, previously hidden by the trees, stood in the center of the grove.

The main house was a one-story building made of grayish brown stone and mortar. I was sure it offered a spectacular view of the mountains above and the town below. The other two smaller buildings, Mario explained, were the grainery and the barn. Some horses, a few cattle and sheep grazed in a nearby corral.

As we approached the house, I noticed a group of men, young and old, standing under a tree. Mario waved at them. Mrs. Quintero and her two other children came out as soon as they heard the engine. After brief introductions and greetings, the women took us into the house and showed us to the guest room and adjacent bathroom. Mario and his brother brought the luggage inside.

Mrs. Quintero gave us a quick tour of the house as she pointed out where everything was. From a large window in the living room, we saw Mario in the courtyard talking to the men we had seen when we came in.

"Who are those men?" Dora asked Mrs. Quintero in Spanish.

"Tomato growers," she answered. "Their crops, and ours, were all damaged by hail. The government promised to insure the crops, but now the officials are coming up with all sorts of excuses not to pay the growers. Mario is head of the *sindicato*, so he's trying to see what can be done."

After giving us some time to take a shower and change, Mario's sister tapped on the door to announce that lunch was ready.

An hour later, after complimenting Mrs. Quintero for a delicious lunch and her hospitality, Dora and I followed Mario into his home office to look at a map of the area Mario had drawn for us. An X within a circle marked the spot where the Lecuona ranch was, up on a ridge, about a half kilometer southeast of the Quintero farm.

There was only one paved road up to the ranch, which, according to Mario, was visible almost in its entirety from the Lecuonas's hacienda. The other way in was a steep mountain trail that led up to a cavern, then wound down to the grazing pastures. On that side, the ranch was protected by a tall fence of mesh and barbed wire erected to deter visitors and locals from wandering onto the property.

"There are two vans, usually with one man per vehicle. They patrol the property. If we need to go in undetected, our best bet is the mountain trail," he recommended. "It's possible to reach the cavern on horseback, but we'd have to go on foot the rest of the way."

"But it's also the longest way," Dora remarked. "What if we can't wait?" she asked.

"If need be, we'll all go in through the front," Mario said.

"Do they know you there?" I asked.

"I know the guards. They're rejects from the Grupo," he answered.

"Are they armed?" Dora asked.

"Of course. Which is why people in town are suspicious of the Lecuonas. You have to understand that in Tepoztlán we don't even have a police force."

"Wow!" Dora exclaimed. "What do people do if they have a police emergency?"

"They rely on their neighbors and friends," Mario answered.

"So our backup is your friend, the violin-making archeologist," she said. He answered with a nod.

"I suppose no one uses guns either," she said.

"Some people own guns but hardly use them," Mario replied.

"You mentioned on the phone that you could supply us with them if necessary," I said.

"I have them." Mario reached in his pocket for a key, walked up to a small armoire, and unlocked it. "Choose your weapons, ladies. And a holster if you'd like."

Dora and I looked in the armoire. There were a number of handguns of different makes and calibers, a shotgun, and a rifle.

"I haven't seen one of these in years," Dora said, taking out a pistol. "*My little Mamba*, my father used to call it. He owned one."

"What did . . . does your father do?" Mario asked.

"Did. He was a career Navy officer," she answered.

"A Navy brat, eh?" Mario remarked.

"That's me," Dora said inspecting the gun. "Yep. I think I'll take this one."

"I'll take that Bauer," I said. I felt a chill go up my spine as I reached for the pistol. No matter how many times I'd held a gun, it still felt cold and strange in my hand until my skin and mind adjusted to it. Then, the gun became an extension of my hand and the caliber of my conscience.

"It's a beauty. Don't you think?" Mario said.

"In a deadly sort of way."

Mario nodded then asked, "Have you used one before?"

"Yes. My partner has one, custom-made. He's let me practice with it."

"I thought you and Dora were partners."

"We're a team only for this case," I explained. "Not that we couldn't be partners. I think she's a pretty good operative."

"I like her, too. Very much," Mario said, throwing a furtive admiring look at Dora, who, at that moment, was trying on a shoulder holster.

"I think we better split up," Mario suggested when we decided to search the town, hoping to locate Licia before she did anything foolish.

Mario decided to make inquiries at the hotels and inns where Licia might be staying. Dora chose to survey the area around the marketplace and main church. I took the northeastern part of the downtown area. It included the Church of the Holy Trinity—La Santísima—and part of the narrow steep path up the mountain to the pyramid that had been the temple of the god Tepoztecatl.

I walked into the crowded church. I heard a woman's loud prayer and her sobbing. I made my way down the main isle and spotted a supplicant. She knelt alone, isolated from the rest. Perhaps out of respect for her pain, people formed a wide circle around her. She prayed in Nahuatl, with her arms stretched out and her teary eyes fixed on the Holy Trinity rising above the altar.

I, too, gazed upon the statue. As usual, the Son and the Holy Ghost were represented by the cross and the white dove, but the artist's rendition of God the Father broke with Western tradition. The artist—a native craftsman, no doubt—had depicted the Father as a man with high cheekbones and arched brows, large slanted eyes, and a long straight moustache hanging down each side of his mouth—a god deserving of a prayer in Nahuatl or Chinese.

"Hello, Jade-eyed God," I said under my breath. Suddenly, I felt uneasy, as if someone were watching me. I turned around and met the stare of a woman, standing a short distance behind me.

She was dressed in black, her head and mouth covered by a black *rebozo*. It had to be Licia, I thought, but soon realized my mistake, for this other woman was taller and heavier than her. When she saw me looking at her, the woman headed for the front door of the church. I rushed out after her.

She walked fast, past the crafts and the food stands lining the stone-covered Santísima Street on each side. The street divided up ahead, so I stopped briefly to check the map of the area Mario had drawn for me. I was faced with two possibilities, the narrow, steep path up to the pyramid, the House of the Tepozteco, or another trail skirting around the *ojo de agua*, a natural spring. But when I looked down the street again, the woman in black had disappeared.

I was getting ready to start the climb to the pyramid, when I felt a tap on my shoulder. I turned my head and saw the woman in black behind me. Half of her face was still covered by the *rebozo*, but I recognized her eyes.

"Isabela?" I asked, but the woman didn't answer.

She signaled for me to follow her. When we reached an isolated spot, Isabela Logorreta uncovered her face.

"I'm sorry about this charade. I had to be sure no one saw me." Before I had a chance to respond, she quickly added, "I called you, but the woman who answered said you had plans to climb up to the Tepozteco. I knew it'd be hours before you got back. So I decided to try to find you. Soon after I got home, Licia showed up. She demanded to talk to Inés and Martín. They were still at the market, but my husband and my father were home, entertaining some investors from Cuernavaca and Mexico City who are planning to build a resort and a golf course outside Tepoztlán. Licia refused to leave. My husband was afraid that she might cause trouble in front of his guests, so he ordered one of the guards to take Licia to a room in the back of the house. He promised her that she would see the children as soon as they got home. He and my father took their business guests to lunch at El Ciruelo, a restaurant across from the marketplace.

"But, before Juan left, I overheard him tell the guard to take

Licia to the cave. They would deal with her later this evening. Something awful is going to happen. I know it," Isabela said with a quavering voice. Grabbing my arm, she pleaded, "Help me."

I patted her hand, then took out my map of the area. Pointing at the cave above the Lecuona Hacienda, I asked, "Is this the cave?" When she nodded, I said, "But I understand people visit that cave. Why would your husband take a chance on anyone walking in on them?"

"There's another entrance to that cave; it's part of our property. Actually, they are two separate caves that connect through a long passage. A gate keeps visitors away from our side. You see, Juan and my father use the cave to store . . . things."

"The pre-Columbian artifacts and jewels they smuggle out of Mexico." I kept my thoughts about their drug-smuggling to myself.

Isabela lowered her head.

"Go back home and try to stay calm," I said. "Maybe you and your children can go to Cuernavaca or some other place."

"I can't. Juan wants me there. One of his guests is staying with us. I have this terrible feeling that he's planning to make Martín 'deal' with . . ." Isabela broke down and dropped to her knees.

"You have to be strong," I said, helping her up. "Your children need you more than ever."

Isabela reached into her dress pocket and took out a key. "You'll need this," she said as she handed it to me. Draping her *rebozo* over her nose and mouth, she rushed down the street.

TWENTY-EIGHT
Dark Tops, False Bottoms

As soon as we got back to the farm, Mario and his brother went to saddle the horses. Dora and I checked and packed our gear, and put fresh batteries in the flashlights. As a precaution, I tied two extra cells together with a large rubber band and put them in my jacket pocket, together with a couple of extra clips. Dora did the same. I looked for my compass and the chain I used to wear it. I slid the chain through the key Isabela had given me and hung it around my neck. I clipped the holster to my belt, and secured the Bauer in it. Dora and Mario decided to take small ankle guns as well.

When Dora saw the horse she was to ride, she took a few steps back. The expression on her face reminded me of my uneasiness when I first mounted a horse at age twelve.

"You'll ride with me, then," Mario said to Dora. "How about you, Gloria? Will you be all right?"

"I'll be okay," I said, hoping that it would all come back to me soon enough.

"Remember, if we are not back in two hours, call Miguel at the violin shop. He'll know what to do," Mario told his brother as we rode out.

We rode at a good stride through the ploughed fields, then turned onto the stone and gravel trail that led to the cave. My horse shuddered and whinnied a little as its hoofs touched the hard stone ground. But it soon stepped up to the task again.

Every so often, we had to stop to let through a few pedestrians walking down the mountain, fewer as we ascended. The sun was beginning to set behind the peaks on the other side of Tepoztlán, illuminating the eastern ridges of the sierra. Although the evening air felt crisp and invigorating, I was sure the night was going to be much colder. For the time being, my mind found comfort in the twittering of birds and the cooing of doves, seeking the refuge of their nests. But an owl's hoot sent a chill up my spine as I remembered my vision at Rosa's house and Mami Julia's old proverb, "When the owl hoots, the Indian dies." My heart stepped up its pace as if to remind me that hope still ran through my veins, red and warm.

As we came to a bend on the road, I saw the mouth of the cave clearly and pulled the reins slightly, making my horse slow down. My breathing quickened. There was something about going into a cave that excited me. Perhaps it was simply the allure of the unknown. I prompted my horse to move on. A short while later, we turned onto a very narrow trail which ended on a large patch of tall, pale yellow grass. We dismounted and tied the horses to a tree, loosely, so they could graze.

"What now?" Dora said, rubbing her thighs then stretching her legs.

"Now, we wait until we're sure everyone has left," Mario answered.

"I don't think there's anyone left," Dora said. "We haven't seen anyone going down the trail in the last twenty minutes."

"The cave attendant is still there. He's a friend, but I don't want to explain what we're doing here. He and I used to play in this cave. He'll be leaving soon. Then we can go in," Mario said.

"Good. I'm going to go behind those bushes and pee," Dora said. "Are you coming, Gloria?"

"Sure. I'll go with you."

When we got back to the spot, Mario said, "Get ready. The attendant is leaving."

We waited until the man was out of sight. Dora and I took our flashlights out of the backpack on my horse and followed Mario into the cave.

The chamber was ample, and its inner wall glittered as the rays of the setting sun shone directly on it. The ground felt solid under my feet as we followed the trail thousands of people had treaded before us. Cows, dogs, horses, symbols and sketchy human figures in different positions were carved on rocks along the walls.

"Wow," Dora and I whispered as the narrow beams of our flashlights partly illuminated the intricate formations water had sculpted on the walls and ceiling of the inner cavern.

The darkness grew denser and the odor of moist earth stronger. I'd always liked the darkness, although I'd never been in a place so dark as the inner chamber. But the hardest part was getting used to an environment so devoid of sound, where an occasional sigh from my companions was as welcomed as a musical arpeggio. People had compared being in a cave to being back in the womb. But it wasn't so. Unlike a mother's heart to her unborn baby, the Earth's heartbeat was inaudible to me.

"Now, which of these do we take?" Dora asked Mario as we got to the end of the chamber and faced the openings to two separate passages. Both of them were chained with warning signs that read *PROHIBIDO EL PASO*.

Checking my compass, I realized that we were still facing east. We would have to walk south to reach our destination. Not knowing which of those tunnels went in that direction, I had no suggestion to offer.

Mario aimed his light at the area above each of the openings. Each had a figure carved on a stone. They resembled the shape of some of the mountains I'd seen around there. Long ago, I surmised, the old Tepoztecos had used those signs to guide themselves through the caverns. There were other signs in Spanish that warned against possible cave-ins.

"This one," Mario said, as he pointed his light at the carving showing a rectangular figure with a circle above it. "Man's Mountain."

We made our way slowly, having at times to crawl through parts of the narrow low tunnel. Just before we got to what seemed a dead end, the sound of running water reached my ears. A great round dark rock blocked part of the way, leaving only enough space for one person of average build to walk on all fours through its four-foot length. Mario crossed over to the other side, then Dora. As I side stepped through it, I put my ear to the rock and heard the resonant sound of running water inside it.

An instant before I got through to the other side, I thought I heard someone say my name. "Yes," I answered softly as I finally reached the spot where Mario and Dora waited for me. I was surprised when they both told me they hadn't said anything. *I do love you*, I heard the same voice say, but this time I knew it was Justin's voice. His face flashed in my mind. I felt the humid warmth of his breath on my hand and saw before me a large wooden crucifix on the wall. I must have been hallucinating again, I thought, as I caught a glimpse of the gate before us.

Mario flashed his light on the wooden gate reinforced with strips of metal. I took out the key Isabela had given me. I gave my flashlight to Dora, who turned mine off and used hers to shed light on the lock. Mario turned his light off, too. I had to jiggle and turn the key a few times before I could unlock it. As we pried it open, the rusty hinges and old wood creaked lightly. I prayed that whoever was on the other side of it would not be alerted to our presence.

Dora handed me my flashlight. I got my gun out of the holster and clicked off the safety. Two other clicks followed mine. At least we were all on the same wavelength, I thought, but that certainty did not help me breathe more easily nor my heart beat more slowly.

"Turn on your lights on the count of one," Mario whispered.

Taking a few steps back, I knelt on one knee. I quickly searched for the on-button of my flashlight with my left hand, as Mario began the countdown to pull the gate completely open.

I held my breath and turned on my light, expecting to see someone standing there with a rifle or shotgun ready to fire. Instead, I saw a number of empty baskets strewn around. The ground showed no signs of footprints or any other disturbance. We still had the element of surprise on our side. I let my breath out and lowered my gun. So did Mario and Dora.

Mario asked us to wait where we were. He wanted to check

the ground ahead.

"I hate playing the role of a damsel in distress," Dora said after a while.

"I do, too," I said. "Let's go."

We caught up to Mario, just as we saw the steady glow of a lantern. Then we proceded cautiously until we had a clearer view of the cave. It was much smaller than the chamber we had gone through on the other side. Small mounds, like large anthills, rose here and there. At first, I thought that they were natural formations. On second look, I noticed that the light from the lantern, which shone evenly on the small hills, didn't shed any light on some areas next to them.

"Someone has been doing some digging here," I whispered to Mario and Dora. "Those are piles of dirt and the dark areas next to them are holes. Be careful."

With their guns in their hands, Mario and Dora scurried farther into the chamber and hid behind the highest dirt piles. I left the Bauer in the holster and crawled my way towards them.

At the far end, through the open mouth of the cave, I could see a light or two flicker in the distance. Then, I saw Licia resting against the wall with her knees bent and her arms behind her back. A man sat next to her in a similar position. I surmised that he was Don Remigio, Bernardina's uncle and Licia's guide from Coyoacán. Beside them, I saw a number of large wooden crates. Another man, who I assumed was the guard Isabela had mentioned, was putting some pottery into one of the crates. He was wearing dark clothes and a gun, cowboy style. His shotgun lay on the edge of a crate next to a large bottle of Coca-Cola.

I rushed to my companions' side and briefed them on my findings. Mario signaled for Dora and me to go in opposite directions to form a circle. He took the center. I took the Bauer out of the holster. Not losing sight of Mario and Dora, or of the guard with his back to us, I inched my way to the mound closest to Licia and Don Remigio. Taking a quick look in the long but narrow trench next to me, I saw two large plastic bags, one tied up with a nylon cord, the other open. I reached in, pulled out a a few dry leaves and smelled them. For a drug-dealer I was sure that was a treasure, but not pre-Columbian.

As I took a step back, I heard a crunching sound, which seemed to be coming from Mario's direction. I threw a quick glance at the guard, ready to stand up and fire if necessary. To our surprise, he kept on packing the crates, seemingly oblivious to the noise, stopping every so often to take a sip of his Coca-Cola.

Out of the corner of my eye, I saw Mario trying to get my attention. He pointed at the guard then at himself to indicate he was going in first.

The guard turned, and I noticed the earphones and the wires connecting to the radio-cassette player clipped to his belt. I gave thanks to Saint Christopher's replacement in heaven for listening to my mother's prayers.

Just as the guard picked up a large pot, Mario and I stood up and pointed our guns at him. So did Dora, a short distance behind him.

The guard dropped the clay pot at seeing Mario and me, but he took no notice of Dora behind him. He reached down as if to get his gun, but his hand stopped mid-way. His panic-stricken eyes moved rapidly from Mario to me, then to the shotgun on the crate. Dora put her gun on the ground and lunged towards him. The impact brought him down flat. She sat on his back, pinning his shoulders under her knees, then reached back and took his gun out of the holster. Pointing it at the back of his head, she warned, "*No te muevas.*" I doubted the man could hear her warning, for he still had the headphones wrapped around his head.

I put the Bauer back in the holster and rushed to get the shotgun. Dora got off the man's back and Mario pulled him up to his feet with one hand.

"*¿Dónde están los otros?*" Mario shouted, his face close to the man's face.

"*Vete a la chingada,*" the man answered in a loud voice. His face was red, but the adrenaline pumping through his body at full speed was making him shake. He threw a glance at the shotgun in my hand, and I felt the prick of fear on the back of my neck. I took a few steps back, but he made a move towards me anyway. Holding the gun by the barrel with both hands, I raised it, ready to strike him. But Dora was faster than me. She struck him hard on the back with the butt of his own gun. He dropped to his knees. A second blow to the back of his neck flattened him again.

"Better this way," she said. Her movements had been quite deliberate and she seemed calm. But the sweat running down her cheeks and the slight trembling of her hand as she handed the gun to Mario betrayed her fear.

Mario gave her his handkerchief. After wiping her face with it, she knelt down to check on the man. "He's alive," she said. Then, she slid the earphones off the guard's head and put one of them to her ear.

"Saved by Barry Manilow," she said. "That's why he couldn't hear all the racket you made." For the first time since he'd met us at the airport, a wave of red lapped at Mario's cheeks.

I left them to work out their disenchantments and rushed to Licia's side. After a brief glance at me, she lowered her eyes and kept her gaze fixed on the ground as I loosened her gag and untied her, then Don Remigio.

"Use these to tie him up," I told Mario, throwing the pieces of rope I had just taken off Licia.

Using one of the crates as support, Licia got up slowly. She finally looked at me, but said nothing. I could still read in her eyes her unrelenting determination. That worried me. She began to look into the crate next to her. I helped Don Remigio to get up, but he was too weak to stand up and he collapsed.

"Keep an eye on him," I told Licia when I saw Mario walk towards the mouth of the cave. He saw me and signaled for me to stay behind him. Walking with my back against the wall, I followed him closely until he reached the opening. Cautiously, he stuck his head out and looked around. "All clear," he said, turning around. "We should get going. We'll go back the way we came."

"I don't think the old man can make it. And Licia is going to be a handful," I told him. "Is there another way?"

"We're looking at it," he replied, pointing at the opening of the cave.

"What's down there? The main house?"

"The road stops a few feet down. There are probably steps up to this cave. We can negotiate those quickly, I think. But the open field below is what worries me. We'll have to skirt around it and go through the underbrush. Then, we'll have to make a dash through another open area, and, hopefully, reach the stables. After that, I don't know. As Mrs. Legorreta told you, they are entertaining that VIP from Mexico City. I know for a fact he's a friend of Raúl Salinas de Gortari, the President's brother. I also know that he travels with two bodyguards. He might spare one if Legorreta or Lecuona tells him what's going on. I'm hoping that their guest knows nothing about this. And unless Mrs. Legorreta squealed, they might not even know we're here."

"So we're talking about Legorreta, his own guard and possibly a loaned one, not counting young Martín. We'll have to risk it, or even out the odds," I said. "What about your friend the archeologist-violin maker? Wasn't he part of Plan B?"

"Yes. But he and a couple of other friends are supposed to wait for us down the road from the hacienda." Mario looked at his watch. "We have less than an hour to get down there. I don't think we can make it. The old man is going to slow us down."

"Let's try. It seems to me we have no other choice," I suggested and went back into the cave.

Mario and I rummaged around the items on a long workshop table next to the crates. He found a half-eaten taco which he tossed away. In a rusty first aid box, I found a few bandages, some antibiotic cream and a small bottle of analgesic tablets.

"Is that aspirin?" Mario asked.

I looked at the bottle and nodded. He took the bottle, popped its cap and dropped four of the white tablets onto his open palm. "Get me the bottle of Coca-Cola," he said. He made Don Remigio take the tablets and gulp down the Coke. The older man gagged but kept on drinking. "That might do the trick."

While Mario explained to Don Remigio what we had to do, I went to tell Dora about the change of plans. She had tied up, gagged and blinded the guard and was busy breaking some of the large jars and examining their bottoms. Sitting on a crate nearby, Licia watched Dora's every move with eager eyes.

"Pretty clever," Dora said, showing me the jar the guard had dropped. "They make a copper base, tape the pre-Columbian jewels to the bottom of the base, then fill it with sand. These copper strips around the base and from the base to the top of the jar hold everything together. Pointing at some other pots, she continued, "Those larger ones contain flat packages of marijuana. I'd say about a pound of the weed in each. My guess is that they use the jars to transport the *mota* and the artifacts in cars or trucks. As to how they get them to their final destination, your guess is as good as mine."

"Let the cavalry figure it out," I said, referring to Mario's friend, the archeologist. "We'd better get going." I briefly outlined the change in plans. Mario found another lantern, a box of matches, and a long piece of rope. Making a loop, he tied both ends around the neck of the lantern, and slid it over his shoulder. He also took a box of matches.

"Just in case we need to set a fire," he said.

"Let's go," I told Licia. "And please, no more surprises."

We were at the mouth of the cave, ready to go down the steps, when I took another look at the road down below. "It's too late. We'll have to go back through the cave," I said. Headlights moved towards us like the unblinking eyes of an ocelot closing in on its prey.

TWENTY-NINE
Two Mothers, One Destiny

Mario headed the group, with Don Remigio right behind him, then Licia and me followed by Dora. The older man seemed more energetic and was able to keep up with the rest of us.

"They're there," Dora whispered when we all heard the echo of clatter and loud voices in the cave behind us. We walked faster until we reached the gate. I handed Mario the key to unlock it. He pushed it with his foot, stepped beyond it, and held it open until we all had walked through the opening. Then he locked it again and put the key back in his jacket pocket.

We moved fast and squeezed through the opening between the rock and the wall. I remembered the difficult crossing through the low, narrow passage ahead of us, and I knew the worst was yet to come. Just before Dora and I dropped to our knees to crawl through the tunnel, we heard the reverberations of a loud noise. Clumps of dirt and small rocks fell on our heads.

"They got through," Dora said, under her breath.

When we heard it again, I realized the sound was made by something hitting the wooden gate. "No. They're trying to break it down. I hope they don't try to blast their way through with a shotgun or this will be our tomb and theirs," I told Dora. I knew it wouldn't take Legorreta long to figure out we'd had inside help. But it was too late to worry about Isabela's safety. I kept moving.

As we approached the end of the passage, Don Remigio collapsed again.

"I can't give him any more aspirin," Mario said, shaking his head. The ceiling was too low for Mario to carry Don Remigio over his shoulder. Crouching and taking a few steps back at a time, he dragged Don Remigio through the passage.

We reached the end of the Man's Mountain tunnel, where we had first entered, then stepped onto the floor of the inner chamber.

"No se preocupen por mí," Don Remigio said, as Dora and Mario propped him up against the wall of the chamber. While Mario and I checked our surroundings, trying to come up with a plan, the older man told Dora and Licia that he knew how to use a gun: We should just give him one and leave him there. He apologized for not being able to do more for us. He owed us his life for however long he hoped to have it.

We all knew the old man made sense. Reluctantly, we agreed to his request. Helping him up, Mario took him to the opening of the second passage, next to the Man's Mountain tunnel we had taken into the Lecuona cave. There, he could keep out of sight more easily. Dora gave him the guard's gun, a .357, and told him what he had to do. Licia watched and listened attentively to Dora's directions. Mario removed the lantern from his neck and handed it to the man along with the box of matches, advising him to use it only if needed.

"Why don't you all stay here and let me go alone," Licia suggested, apologizing for putting us in harm's way. "After all, they want me, not you."

"That's no longer true," Dora rebutted. "They already know who we are and how many weapons we have."

"We're wasting precious time. It's better if you come with us," I told Licia. She turned around and went to look after the older man.

Mario, Dora and I found a strategic place behind some formations in the chamber, but still close enough to the Man's Mountain passage. From there, we could more easily spot or hear anyone moving through the large, dark cave in front of us. We crouched close to each other. Dora put her flashlight in a cleft between two small mounds. She pointed its beam down towards us so we could glimpse one another as we talked.

"As I see it, they'll be waiting outside the cave, where they can take us down one by one, although they run the risk of one of us getting away," I said.

"I agree," Dora said.

"Okay. We'll go separate ways," Mario said. "Spread out. Don't follow the open path. Stay close to the walls. I hope you remember some of the layout because we might not be able to use the flashlights. If they're not in the cave, we'll have to wait, but we'll have an advantage. When we get to the mouth of the cave, wait ten minutes." Mario paused briefly to catch his breath, then continued, "Keep track of time anyway you can. If they're outside, then, I'll go out first. If I make it, I'll signal you."

"How?" Dora asked.

"Two short hoots," he replied. "Then you go, Gloria. Then you, Dora. Go out shooting. If the worst happens, your client is on her own."

"I'm no owl," Dora said. "I'll have to whistle."

My soul cringed and my breath left me for a second at the foreboding memory of the owl's cry.

Dora went to get Licia. "I think it's better if Licia comes with me. We'll follow you, Mario. She and I will be the last ones to get out."

I agreed. Unable to keep still any longer, I took the Bauer out of the holster. Hiding behind the rock formations, I circled around until I found the wall. I assumed Dora, Licia and Mario were doing the same.

The darkness was oppressive now, but the silence was as light to bear as hope. To keep my mind busy, I began to keep track of the time. It would take us at least twenty minutes to get to the opening, then we were to wait another ten minutes. With my back to the wall, I moved as quickly as possible, then crawled the last few feet towards the mouth of the cave.

The darkness grew lighter and I could see the silhouette of trees and a few blinking lights in the distance. My eyes moved quickly through the underbrush around the base of the trees. Nothing stirred. *Minus five minutes*, I counted. I closed my eyes for a few seconds. Bits and pieces of conversations with my daughter and mother, with Darío and with Justin came flashing through my mind. All the grief, all the anger and every other emotion I had ever felt seemed to have formed stagnant pools in my ears, blocking the air from leaving to make room for sound. But there was no sound to be heard, I reminded myself, just the frantic pulse of my life at that moment. I was at the mouth of a cave, alone with my memories and my fears.

I heard footfalls outside the cave. Anxiously, I looked across the way for Mario and Dora and breathed more easily when I heard Mario call my name softly. I whispered a "yes." Dora and Licia had to be close by, but I couldn't see or hear them.

Minus three minutes, I counted mentally, as I heard muffled voices outside. I shifted my position until I was facing the opening. I held my breath and listened attentively. The voices of two men were coming from my left. I hoped Mario and Dora had also heard them.

Dora and Licia made a quick dash across the opening of the cave and joined me. "We go on as planned," Dora whispered in my ear. She'd hardly finished her sentence when I saw Mario lunge out of the cave. He fired his shotgun once. A flashlight went on, followed by six shots.

"A single shooter. I think . . . I hope he missed Mario," Dora said between short breaths.

"No. There are at least two men out there," I told Dora.

Without warning, Dora stood up, aimed, and fired repeatedly at the flashlight, putting it out. I heard a man's scream. She had hit more than the flashlight. Contrary to what I expected, the cave seemed to have absorbed the noise of the shots. Their echo bounced off the walls and rock formations, losing strength somewhere in the inner tunnels. I heard Licia mutter something I couldn't understand. Then, there was silence.

We listened for Mario's signal, but no owl hooted. An instant later, we heard a man say, "Throw out your guns and come out with your hands up. We'll let you go." I knew the man out there wasn't Legorreta. "We know how many guns you have, so no tricks," the man warned.

I was beginning to wonder why Legorreta wasn't the one

talking, when Dora whispered in my ear, "Thank God Mario gave me his gun before I joined you. And there is no way they know about my extra gun. He's going by what the guard told them."

Since Mario had fired the shotgun, whoever was out there must have thought that we had four guns left. Counting Dora's extra gun and Mario's, we had exactly that number, since we had left the .357 with Don Remigio. Given the odds, if we threw them all out, we would surely be handicapped.

"One of the flashlights," Dora suggested, "It would roll. Hardly the sound of a gun sliding over the ground."

"I've got it. My compass, I said, as I took off my chain. My hands were trembling when I unlocked it and I slid the compass out. My compass was made of heavy pewter, but still light enough not to sound like a gun sliding on rocky soil. So I took out the batteries, loosened the rubber band, removed one, and pushed the compass under the other. "Okay, throw your gun first, then I'll throw the compass and mine out."

"*Here they go,*" Dora shouted. Licia said something in Nahuatl. I prayed that she wasn't about to have an episode similar to the one at her house.

Licia had quieted down when Dora shoved the first gun out and counted. Heaven was still on our side, I thought: They were not using their flashlights to make sure those were indeed weapons. I crawled closer to the cave opening, and lying on my stomach, I pushed the compass out and let it slide on the ground. Dora counted aloud. There was no response. As I threw the Bauer out I heard two short but loud hoots.

"Mario," Dora said behind me. I prayed she was right, that it was not a real owl waiting for my soul.

The man said, "Throw the last one and come out with your hands up."

The beam of a large flashlights went on suddenly, blinding us. Instinctively, we retreated into the darkness.

"I guess he feels the odds are in his favor now," Dora said.

As we saw the flashlight moving towards us, we heard the whinnying of a horse. The beam shifted direction. At the sound of galloping hoofs, the flashlight crashed on the ground. A rifle shot thundered down the mountain. But the horse was already upon the shooter. I saw the flash of a second shot, then a third and fourth. My breath left me. A man screamed. A body hit the ground. A horse galloped down the mountain. My heart rushed after him.

Suddenly, I sensed someone very close to me. I turned ready to fire.

"Give me your flashlight," Mario said.

With a sigh of relief, I picked up my flashlight and handed it to him. From his vantage point, he surveyed the area outside. His rifle next to him, the guard's body lay on the ground, motionless. We waited. Backed up by Dora and me, Mario decided to check the scene outside. He came back with all the guns but not my compass.

"I found the body of the other guard down below, but no sign of the professor or his son," Mario said.

"Licia!" I exclaimed, as I pointed my flashlight around. "She's gone."

"What?" Dora asked.

"Legorreta. The gate," I replied as I began to run towards the inner chamber. Not knowing exactly what was going on, Dora and Mario ran after me. They soon caught up to me.

"Get down," Mario said when we saw the soft glow of Don Remigio's lantern suddenly grow stronger.

Hiding behind the formations, we approached the spot. I sneaked a look. Closer to the opening of the Man's Mountain passage, I saw Don Remigio and the Legorretas. I gasped. Martín had one of his arms wrapped around the old man's chest. With his right hand—the same hand I'd seen in my vision—he pointed a pistol at Don Remigio's temple. There was no sign of Licia. I prayed that she was hiding somewhere, safe.

When I looked at the group again, I saw Isabela step out of the Man's Mountain tunnel.

"What are you doing here?" Legorreta asked.

"I won't let you do this to my children," she said, at the top of her lungs. "Come with me, Martín."

Martín seemed confused but didn't ease his grip on Don Remigio or lower his gun.

Isabela's command to her son was followed by a barrage of insults from Legorreta. Isabela answered him with a few harsh words of her own. He shoved her, and she fell to the ground. I could no longer see her, but I could hear her sobbing.

"You three out there. I know you're there. I've been expecting you. Come out in the open," Legorreta said. "Do it or he dies."

Faced with such a predicament, we put our weapons back in their holsters. Mario threw the rifle out to gain some time and test Legorreta's determination. When he didn't fire, we stood up with our arms raised.

"Come closer," the professor said.

When we did as told, he said, "Good. Now, open your coats and slowly take your guns out. Toss them to the side, far, one at a time."

We followed his command. Our only hope rested on Dora's and Mario's ankle pistols. As if he were talking to his students at the university, every time we followed his instructions, Legorreta expressed his approval with a "Good."

Not sure that those were all the weapons we carried, Legorreta told us to take off our jackets and turn around. My arms ached at the contact with the cold air.

"Put your coats back on. We wouldn't want you to catch cold now," Legorreta said in a sarcastic tone. A little man with a big gun, he was enjoying his power play.

Satisfied, Legorreta said, "Turn that bitch over to me and you can all walk out of here, this old man included."

I knew that Licia was somewhere in the vicinity. I took furtive looks around and finally spotted a piece of her dress in the opening of the passage where we had left Don Remigio. I had no idea how she had managed to get there and hide. I nudged Dora's elbow, then took her hand and raised it, pointing it in Licia's direction. She squeezed my hand in response.

"C'mon," Legorreta said. "You're trying my patience."

Licia came out of the passage, holding the .357 with both hands. Slowly, I lowered my head. As unobtrusively as possible, I kept an eye on her. She walked as fast as she could, keeping close to the wall behind Legorreta. If lucky, she would be standing right behind him in a short time.

Isabela, who had quieted down, rose to her feet slowly. She looked in Licia's direction, then at us.

"Where is the bitch?" Legorreta said, furious at our silence.

Unexpectedly, Isabela threw herself at her husband's legs and pleaded, "Stop it! Stop it!"

Taken by surprise, he stumbled but regained his balance immediately. He tried to shake Isabela off, but she hung on to him tightly. Licia moved closer. Legorreta lowered his arm and grabbed Isabela by the hair. Martín eased his grip on Don Remigio and looked down to check on his mother, but he didn't release the older man altogether. Isabela let go of her husband's legs and tried to get herself free.

"Let her go," Licia said, almost right behind him.

Legorreta turned slightly to look at her over his shoulder, releasing Isabela. She grabbed him and pulled him down. He stumbled back.

Dora and Mario reached down to get their ankle guns. I made a dash for mine. Panic-stricken, Martín let go of the old man. Don Remigio collapsed to the ground, but began to crawl out of the way.

Martín took a few steps back, pointing his gun at us, then at Licia. "You killed my father. You took him from me," he said to her.

Licia threw her head back as if hit by a stone. I gasped as if a projectile had also hit my chest. As I suspected, he had known all along that Licia was his mother. What else had Legorreta said to his son? How had this monster convinced Martín to attempt the murder of his own mother?

I heard Licia tell Martín, "You don't understand. Peter, your father, was going to kill me. He wanted to kill you and Inés, too. I couldn't let him do that. I loved your father. I love you. Please, put your gun down." She was almost out of breath, and her hand was shaking.

Legorreta, who had been pulled down by Isabela, got to his feet quickly, as Martín told Licia, "You're lying." Turning to Legorreta, he said, "She's lying, isn't she?"

"She's a liar," Legorreta replied. "Kill her! Shoot!"

"Don't do it, Martín. Don't," Isabela said.

Legorreta kicked his wife hard in the head.

Martín's eyes shifted from Licia to Legorreta then to Isabela, now lying motionless on the ground. Terrified and confused, Martín lowered his arm, but didn't drop his weapon.

"Put down your guns," Legorreta told us. "Yours, too," he said, turning to Licia. When she wouldn't heed, he said, "You don't and I'll kill your son." He pointed the gun at Martín.

Cursing him, Licia dropped her gun. Legorreta kicked the gun out of the way and looked in our direction. "Now, yours. C'mon, c'mon. Throw them over here."

I threw mine, but before Dora and Mario had a chance to do anything, Martín raised his left arm and pointed the gun at his father, then slowly began to turn the gun towards himself.

"No," Licia shouted as she lunged towards her son.

Legorreta hesitated. Dora aimed and fired, but he had already pulled the trigger.

Without thinking, I ran towards Licia. The bullet from Legorreta's gun had missed her but not Martín. Thrown back by the impact, and with Licia's weight on him, he stumbled backwards with his arms stretched out and his finger still on the trigger. I saw the flash from Martín's gun as his body hit the ground. An arrow of fire pierced my flesh, burning everything in its path through my left thigh then up my belly. I wondered who was screaming, not realizing the scream was rolling out of my own mouth. I reeled back. I felt a sharp pain on the back of my head as I hit the ground. A hot stream ran down my belly, and I reached down to touch my thigh. I looked at my fingers, full of blood. *An earthquake,* I thought, as I felt the trembling of the ground underneath me.

I turned my head, looking for the faces I knew were there, but all I could see was the sign of Man's Mountain above the dark mouth of the passage. A halo formed around the circle that was the man's head. It became my daughter Tania's face, glowing brighter, then spiraling until it became a single point of light, swiftly receding into the swelling darkness in my head.

THIRTY
Black Widow's Dwelling

"Love is a small patch of soil where we grow flowers," Mami Julia was telling me. "The idea, you see, is to grow as many flowers as you can before you move on to another patch." We were looking at her tiny garden in our house in Jingle Town.

In my dream, I was an adult, but I was wearing a white gown similar to my First Communion dress.

"Why are you reminding me of all that now? Am I dead?" I asked her. She only smiled at me and held my hand. I could feel the humid warmth of her skin on mine.

I opened my eyes. The light trickling in through a window blinded me. I tried to shield my eyes from it, but I seemed to lack the strength to raise either of my hands. I closed my eyes again and said, "I want to go back, Mami Julia. I didn't say goodbye."

"Shhh," someone whispered in my ear. "I'm here. You don't have to say goodbye," a man's voice said. Thinking that I was still dreaming, I turned my head towards his voice and opened my eyes again. The first thing I saw was a large crucifix on the wall, then Justin looking at me. He had dark circles under his eyes, as if he hadn't slept for days, but he smiled. I tried to sit up, but pain stabbed at my left side, robbing me of breath. Panting, I lay back.

"Doctor," I heard a woman say. *"Ya está despierta."*

A young man wearing a white coat rushed to my side, followed by a nurse. "Do you know where you are?" he asked with a heavy accent.

"No," I replied. "Should I?"

He smiled. "Do you remember what happened?" He beamed a light into my eyes and took my pulse.

The events in Tepoztlán came rushing in like the waters of a flooding river. Pain stabbed at my side again. Justin came closer and took my hand in his. "I was shot," I answered, trying to touch my wound with my free hand.

Taking my hand away from the injured area, the doctor answered, "You're in a hospital in Cuernavaca. You had extensive surgery."

"How extensive?"

"You lost much blood before you came here," the doctor said. He paused, groping for the right words in English. "The projectile perforated your spleen. I'm afraid we had to extract your spleen. We had to stop the blood. Also, you had a small fracture in your femur, and a . . . big cut on the back of your neck. You hit your head on a pointed rock when you fell, yes?" he explained. "You had to be transported to this hospital. That made it worse. The doctors in Tepoztlán didn't have the equipment to treat your kind of injury. They injected antibiotics and pain-killers, which is good, because you are . . . were trying to get up and leave. You said you had to go back to California because you didn't say goodbye."

I looked at Justin and felt the warmth of my blood rushing to my cheeks. "The others?"

"Dora and Mario are all right. They went to Mexico City to pick up Tania and Pita. I was still in LA ready to go back to Oakland. Before going back I called Pita to find out what was going on. She had just gotten a call from Lester Zamora, who had received a fax from Dora Saldaña, telling him what happened. I took the first flight out. Unfortunately, Pita and Tania had a hard time getting a flight out of San Francisco. They had to fly to Guadalajara and take a connecting flight from there to Mexico City. Dora and Mario offered to pick them up at the airport. I stayed with you." He paused. "Licia Lecuona and that man, Remigio, were here until you came out of surgery. I don't know where she is now. Martín and Juan Gabriel Legorreta were buried yesterday morning."

"Yesterday morning? How long have I been here?" I asked. My eyelids were beginning to feel heavy, and I closed my eyes just to rest them. I vaguely remember Justin saying that I'd been in the hospital three days, then the doctor telling me that I needed my rest.

When I opened my eyes again an hour later, Justin was still sitting by my side, holding my hand. "I do love you. Very much," he said. "I wanted to tell you face to face . . . I was so stupid."

It hurt to move, but it would have hurt much more not to reach out to him and hold him in my arms.

The nurse walked gingerly into the room a while later and asked Justin to leave, so she could check the stitches and give me a sponge bath.

"Le traje los periódicos," the nurse told me and put a stack of newspapers on the night table. She held the front page of the *Diario de Morelos* up so I could see it. It showed a photo of Mario and Dora, holding some of the pre-Columbian pieces we had seen in the cave and the two bags of marijuana. My name was also mentioned, she said. The three of us were now *héroes* because we had saved the nation from being looted of its national treasure by the "powerful, thieving drug smugglers, and Legorreta," she quoted from the newspaper.

A while later, my mother and Tania came into the room. They dropped their things on a chair and rushed to my side. I couldn't hold back the tears any longer when I saw them. Neither could they. When we regained our composure, Tania and my mother began to clean my face, brush my hair, and apply rouge to my cheeks. I didn't understand why they were doing all that, but I basked in their love and care.

"I must have looked awful. Thanks, Hon. Thanks, Mom," I said.

"This isn't for Grandma and me, or even for Justin," Tania said, throwing a glance at Justin. "We love you anyway," she continued, "but there is a newspaper photographer who would like to take a photo of the 'three heroes.' The Mayor of Cuernavaca and a government official from Tepoztlán want to thank you personally. The photographer came with them. If that's okay with you."

Hesitant, I looked at Justin who said, "Take the bow. You

deserve it."

After a discreet moment, Dora and Mario came in.

Dora approached my bed. She said nothing at first. In an uncharacteristic manner, she bent over and kissed me on the cheek. Her eyes were moist and she swallowed hard as she said, "You gave us quite a scare, partner." Turning to Justin, she said, "No offense meant, Escobar."

"None taken. Call me Justin."He shook the hand she offered.

"We're so glad you're still with us. I can't tell you how sorry I am you're the one who got hurt," Mario said, coming closer and shaking my hand.

"We have something for you," Dora said, holding up my compass. "It took a while, but we found it, under some bushes."

Words tied up in knots in my throat and tears rushed to my eyes again.

"No need to thank me," Dora said and freshened up my make-up.

The mayor and the photographer walked in a while later. A few pictures were snapped as the government officials shook hands with the three of us and thanked us for our efforts to stop the smuggling of the pre-Columbian artifacts from Tepoztlán. He also told us that a crew of archeologists and curators from Mexico City had arrived in Tepoztlán to further investigate where the archeological sites were and to catalogue all the items found in the cave.

Isabela Legorreta had also agreed to turn in to the Mexican Consulate in San Francisco all the artifacts and jewels in her husband's private collection. In exchange she and her daughter would not be prosecuted and would be allowed to return to the United States. Everyone else in the Lecuona family would be prosecuted to the fullest extent of the law. The Governor of Morelos had so ordered. But no one mentioned the Lecuonas' drug-smuggling operation.

After the city officials and photographer left, Mario explained that all those powerful people and government officials who had befriended and done business with the Lecuonas and Legorretas denied knowing about their illegal activities. They were now claiming to have been fooled by the Lecuonas, as had·everyone else.

Mario left shortly after, promising to come back every day to see me during my convalescence.

"Michael Cisneros and Lester both send their best and said not to worry about your expenses here. They'll take care of everything," Dora said.

"Licia?"

"She's gone," Dora answered. "She gave me a sealed envelope to give to Michael Cisneros. I'm flying back to San Francisco tomorrow. She also asked me to give you these." Dora handed me a small box and an envelope. "I'll miss you, partner. Keep in touch," she said and waved goodbye as she walked out.

I knew I too would miss her. I asked Justin to open the letter that Licia had left for me. He handed me the small box. Then he tore the envelope open and began to read Licia's letter aloud.

> *These belonged to my grandmother. Please accept them as a token of my appreciation for what you did for me and my children, although, in truth, I'll never be able to repay my debt to you. I know that if it had been up to you, Martín wouldn't have died. I also know that if I hadn't interfered, my son would still be alive. I must carry that terrible truth in my heart for the rest of my days. But now at least my daughter has a chance to be happy with Isabela, her true mother. I've prepared a notarized document instructing Michael Cisneros to sell all my assets and property in the States, except for my house on East Twenty-seventh, and to set up a trust for Inés and Isabela. Dora Saldaña has agreed to take the notarized document back to the States and hand it to Michael. As for me, I'll be going back to the place where I was born, to complete the cycle that began*

on my birth nearly five hundred years ago. Our
paths will never cross again, in this life or next,
but my prayers will always be with you.

"It's signed 'Malintzin Tenepal,'" Justin added.

"La Malinche," my mother said. "Do you think that maybe she really is the reincarnation of La Malinche?" she asked. "Look. Like Malinche, Licia married a Spaniard, who not only didn't love her, but mistreated her and was unfaithful to her. She had a son named Martín, who hated her."

"A few coincidences, at best," I said. There had been times when I nearly believed that Licia was the reincarnation of Malinche. But despite everything I knew about her, Licia Román Lecuona had remained an enigma to me.

I opened the box Licia had left for me.

Joy and pain tore at my heart when I saw Licia's *arracadas*, the gold earrings that I had seen her wear every day in the short time I'd known her. I knew what she intended to do and I was tempted to tell Justin to try to stop her, but I didn't.

A week later, when Mario Quintero came in with a newspaper article that talked about a bizarre incident in the Plaza de la Conchita in Coyoacán, I knew she had succeeded. A pile of women's white clothes, bloody but neatly folded, had been found in the small chapel where I knew Malinche had once prayed to her newly found God. But no body had been found. The priest in charge of the small church had no explanation for the gruesome discovery, since the chapel was locked most of the time, and no one but he had keys to it. I could only surmise that Licia had hidden in the chapel and waited until everyone was gone to end her life. I said a prayer for her soul.

After a week, Justin and Tania went back to Oakland. My mother stayed with me until I could travel.

Still curious about seeing the conquistadors after the Procession of the Dead, I asked my mother to tell me what she recalled about that night. As she spoke, I realized that only Licia and I had seen the conquistadors, that my daughter and mother had seen only the *charros*, as Isabela had told me. Although I still resisted believing, I had to admit that I had no explanation for that particular vision.

During my stay in Mexico, and later, already back in Oakland, I suspected that I had lost my dark gift, for I hardly had dreams of any kind, let alone visions.

At times, in the hours of insomnia that sprinkled my long recovery, I had the neurotic notion that my dark gift had been the product of an overactive spleen. When it was taken out, a part of my pysche too had been removed. Ironically, I had always struggled against my dark gift. Now I missed it. More disturbing still was the notion that Rosa Catalino had the power to restore it, to make my soul whole again. I searched for her, but no one ever heard from or saw Rosa again.

In the light of day, I dismissed all those notions as ludicruous. Still, only one vision, or rather the memory of the vision in which I had seen the woman on fire, haunted me. But, since nothing of the sort happened in the next few months, I began to believe that it had also been nothing more than another bad dream.

As soon as I was back on my feet, I went back to Licia's old Victorian on East Twenty-seventh to visit Carmelo and Bernardina, who were still taking care of her house. Thanks to Michael Cisneros, Bernardina had a good chance to get her green card.

A few months later, on a sunny Saturday afternoon in May, I received a postcard from Lester Zamora. Unable to believe that Licia was really dead, he had decided to take an extended leave from work and had gone to Mexico to look for her.

Unlike him, I believed that Licia had committed suicide. I thought about her often and wore every day the *arracadas* she had given me. I was wearing them on a warm, windy Sunday afternoon in mid-October as Justin, my mother and daughter and I watched from my porch as the Oakland hills were being ravaged by a firestorm, equalled in magnitude only by the fire that had consumed San Francisco after the 1906 earthquake.

Towards the evening, compelled by an obscure desire, I got in my car and drove to Licia's Victorian on East Twenty-seventh. As I arrived, I saw a few firefighters, aided by some Oakland police officers, unsuccessfully trying to quench the flames that enshrouded the old house. Some of the neighbors and security guards from the hospital below were hosing the roofs of nearby houses. Despite the strong wind, the fire seemed confined to Licia's house. But everyone living in the vicinity had been evacuated. They gathered at the foot of the hill to hope and pray that their houses were spared.

I moved quickly through the crowd, looking for Carmelo and Bernardina. Since Licia's body had never been found, Michael Cisneros was also convinced that she was still alive, so he had asked them both to stay on to take care of the property. I saw them standing on the steps leading up to the old building at Highland Hospital. Licia's next-door neighbor with his wife and their two dogs stood next to them. The dogs growled at me but seemed to be as stupefied as their owners, who watched the scene in horror.

"What happened?" I asked Carmelo, who stared blankly at me. I shook him a little and repeated my question.

"I . . . don't know," he finally replied. "Bernardina and I went out to take care of some errands. We got back just a few minutes ago."

"It was the woman who set fire to her house," the neighbor's wife said. "I saw her going in just before the fire started."

"What woman?" I asked.

"The woman who always dressed in white. Black Widow," she replied. "Chaka and Cleo began to howl. They almost never do that. So I went out to the yard to check on them. That's when I saw her go in. A few minutes later, I saw the flames. They started on the second floor. But then, just as I was going to call 911, I saw flames *downstairs*, too. How do you explain a fire starting upstairs and downstairs at the same time? I'm telling you, she torched her own house."

"It can't be," I rebutted. "She's been dead almost a year."